"I called you."

The words were out before she could recall them. Humiliation swaddled her, suffocating and frustrating. But she'd said it. She couldn't unsay it any more than he could unhear it. "Over and over. In the beginning, I mean. Left messages for you with your parents. You never once called back."

"We should get going." He reached for the SUV door.

She glared at him. And there it was. The truth of the matter. He'd left, and even when she called, leaving countless messages for him to please, please call her back...he hadn't.

He just left without looking back.

Olivia settled into the passenger seat and buckled her seat belt. She would take his help if it meant finding out what happened to Willy.

But she would never, ever forgive him.

MURDER AT SUNSET ROCK

USA TODAY Bestselling Author

DEBRA WEBB

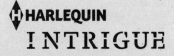

Tennessee has been my home for twenty of the past forty years.
From the birthplace of rock 'n' roll in Memphis to the Great
Smoky Mountains of east Tennessee, it's a wondrous state.
I hope you'll enjoy this second installment of the Lookout
Mountain Mysteries. Sunset Cove is a fictional community
I hope you will enjoy!

HARLEQUIN®
INTRIGUE™

Recycling programs
for this product may
not exist in your area.

ISBN-13: 978-1-335-59031-2

Murder at Sunset Rock

Copyright © 2023 by Debra Webb

Harlequin Enterprises ULC
22 Adelaide St. West, 41st Floor
Toronto, Ontario M5H 4E3, Canada
www.Harlequin.com

Printed in U.S.A.

Debra Webb is the award-winning *USA TODAY* bestselling author of more than one hundred novels, including those in reader-favorite series Faces of Evil, the Colby Agency and Shades of Death. With more than four million books sold in numerous languages and countries, Debra has a love of storytelling that goes back to her childhood on a farm in Alabama. Visit Debra at debrawebb.com.

Books by Debra Webb

Harlequin Intrigue

Lookout Mountain Mysteries

Disappearance in Dread Hollow
Murder at Sunset Rock

A Winchester, Tennessee Thriller

In Self Defense
The Dark Woods
The Stranger Next Door
The Safest Lies
Witness Protection Widow
Before He Vanished
The Bone Room

Colby Agency: Sexi-ER

Finding the Edge
Sin and Bone
Body of Evidence

Faces of Evil

Dark Whispers
Still Waters

Visit the Author Profile page at Harlequin.com.

CAST OF CHARACTERS

Olivia Ballard—A geologist in Montana, Olivia returned to her Tennessee mountain hometown to bury her beloved grandfather.

Huck Monroe—Has been in love with Olivia since he was just a kid. Can he win her back while he solves her grandfather's murder?

Arnold Decker—The Hamilton County sheriff and best friend of the murder victim.

Louis Rogers—A private investigator who is looking for Olivia...but he can't possibly know Olivia.

William Ballard—Olivia's grandfather and an internationally known award-winning photographer. Who would have wanted to hurt him?

Laura Ballard—Olivia's mother who died when Olivia was only four years old. Was she murdered too?

Kasey Aldean—Olivia's father who disappeared the year before her mother died. Has he come back for some sort of revenge?

Chapter One

Firefly LaneSunset Cove, Tennessee
Tuesday, June 6, 4:00 p.m.

Olivia Ballard's fingers tightened on the steering wheel as she slowed for the final turn.

Firefly Lane.

She'd grown up here. At four, when her mother died, her grandparents had carried on with raising her. There was no one else. Her father had disappeared the year before. Olivia drew in a deep breath and made the turn that would take her home. Except was it really home anymore? Everyone was gone.

A fresh wave of tears burned her eyes. Her grandmother—Gran, she had called her—had passed away when she was only nine. Grieved herself to death, Willy, her grandfather, had explained. She never got over losing her daughter, her only child. As much as Gran had loved

Olivia, and Olivia had no doubt that she had, her heart had been fractured beyond repair.

Pushing away the memories, Olivia focused on maneuvering forward. Somehow the long gravel road that cut through the thick woods seemed narrower than the last time she had visited. The thick canopy of trees blocked the sun, leaving the road in an eerie twilight. Half a mile later, the trees parted and the landscape opened up into a lush clearing, rich with the colors of nature. Olivia braked to a stop at the end of the road, which was actually the driveway. Willy's cabin was the only house on Firefly Lane, and it sat at the very end. His land stretched from the road, several acres wide, through the dense forest, over the cliffs and spiraling downward to the world below. As a young girl, Olivia had dared to hike along that cliffside—too close, her Gran would say. Willy would chuckle and tell her to be careful.

Willy, she smiled sadly at the memory of the man she had adored and depended on for everything as an adolescent with no mother or siblings and no grandmother. Everyone had called him Willy—his name was William, after all. No matter how her gran had attempted to prod Olivia into calling him Grandpa or Papa, she had refused. He was Willy. Her father and grandfather all rolled into one. The man who took care of scraped knees and prom dresses and everything in between.

How could he be gone?

Grabbing her cell, Olivia emerged from her car. She tucked the phone into the pocket of her jeans and surveyed the yard. Willy had bordered a full acre around the cabin with a stacked stone fence nearly three feet high. She smiled and shook her head at the idea of just how many stones were required to build that fence. He'd teased her gran often, saying the stone fence was really more of a decoration—remembered from long ago visits to faraway places. Gran would remind him that she had agreed to spend the rest of her life in this mountain cabin of his, but only if he turned it into the cottage of her dreams.

To Olivia, it was very European. With the multitude of flower beds, there were more blooms than grass. A post-and-wire fence surrounded a vegetable garden that would be the envy of gardeners anywhere. Vines snaked up every possible vertical space, including the walls of the house. The place looked more like a hundred-year-old English cottage than a cabin in the woods of Tennessee. Her gran had spent decades creating exactly that look. Even as a little girl, Olivia had known Willy was right about the stone wall being decorative. But that touch had made her gran immensely happy, and Willy would have done anything for her.

Willy's vintage Land Rover Defender was parked next to the house beneath the shade of a massive white oak. A trembling smile tugged at her lips. God, how he'd loved that old thing. He said it made him feel as if he were on safari. Truth was, he carried parts of the world they had visited in his heart too. There were times and places that stayed with you, he would say.

"I should have come back sooner." The words tasted bitter on Olivia's tongue and sank deep into her gut, where they sat like blocks of concrete.

She reached back into the SUV for her bag, then slammed the car door shut, frustration and anger—at herself—burning away the softer emotions. Olivia hadn't been home since Christmas. Christmas! How could she have waited over five months? She and Willy had talked two or three times each week, but that wasn't the same, no matter that they used video chatting most of the time. She should have been *here*.

Now her dear grandfather was dead.

Olivia swiped at the tears that would no longer be held back. Her first stop when she had arrived in Chattanooga had been the Hamilton County Medical Examiner's Office, where she'd insisted on seeing her grandfather's body. Sheriff Arnold Decker, Willy's close friend, had already identified his remains, but Olivia had needed to see for herself that he was really gone. He'd always been so strong and confident. How had this happened?

Her chest tightened with the image that played over and over in her mind. Multiple broken bones and a devastating head injury, the attendant had explained. Her grandfather had fallen, the report said. From Sunset Rock.

Even now, she could hardly believe it was true.

For the past twenty-four hours, Olivia had been operating on autopilot. Late yesterday, the call had come from Sheriff Decker explaining that Willy's body had been found by hikers on Bluff Trail. The assumption was that he'd fallen from the overlook, Sunset Rock. Olivia had heard the words, but her brain had stopped working after the word *dead. Willy is dead.*

On the seemingly endless drive from Bozeman, Montana, she'd repeatedly berated herself for allowing 159 days to pass since she'd hugged him. Since she'd inhaled the familiar woodsy scent of him. She had mentally ticked through each of those days and what she'd done on them, and none of it had been excuse enough not to have visited the only family she had left in this world.

She stared at the house, told herself to move toward it. She was tired. She'd been driving all night—not that sleep would have been possible. Every minute of every hour she'd played Sheriff Decker's words over and over. *I'm so sorry to inform you that your grandfather is dead. When you get here, Liv, you let me know if there is anything I can do to help. I am so, so sorry. He was like a brother to me.*

She had thanked him then ended the call. She hadn't been able to talk...how could Willy be dead?

Even twenty-odd hours later, the little girl in her wanted to crumble to the ground in a sobbing, miserable heap. But she was no little girl anymore. She was thirty years old. A geologist in Bozeman. She owned a townhouse with a mortgage and an SUV. Had work friends.

And no one else. Not a single other person connected to her by blood or anything stronger than the shallowest definition of friendship.

Olivia closed her eyes and forced the horde of debilitating emotions away. She had things to do. When she'd called her boss, she had already been on the road and hadn't been able to say when she would return to work. She had weeks and weeks of unused leave. Her work was well ahead of the rest of the project. It wasn't like she couldn't take a few weeks off. She squared her shoulders. She owed it to Willy to take care of him and his home properly—the way he would want it done.

She dug in her bag for her keys. "No putting this off any longer, Liv."

Forcing one foot in front of the other, she walked to the porch, climbed the three steps and crossed to the door. She poked the key into the lock, took a deep breath and turned it, then opened the door. The scent of home filled her lungs. Her eyes closed with the weight of sensory overload. Didn't matter that she hadn't lived here in a dozen years. Not since college. This would forever be home.

Forcing her eyes open, Olivia stepped inside, closed the door and came to an abrupt halt.

The house was a wreck.

Not merely untidy or cluttered…someone had ransacked the place. Her heart charged into a gallop.

Olivia held her breath. Whoever had done this could still be in the house.

Her icy fingers dove into her bag and closed around the small can of pepper spray Willy had insisted she carry starting the day she left Hamilton County. The spray would be no help against a gun, but it was the only weapon at her disposal just now. She glanced at the shotgun on the rack above the mantel. She listened intently. No sound. Okay, she should make her way to the fireplace and grab that shotgun.

Easing soundlessly in that direction, she kept her gaze roving side to side, checking each door that exited the main room that was living, dining and kitchen all in one. Beyond the first of those doors was a short corridor that led to the bedrooms and bath. The only other door led to a small laundry room and mudroom as well as the back door.

Since the front had been locked, whoever had done this must have entered and, hopefully, departed from the rear of the house.

Olivia made it to the fireplace. Still no sound. No movement. No unexpected odors.

Keeping her attention focused on her surroundings and the spray poised in her right hand, she reached up with her left and clutched the long, cold barrel. She lifted the shotgun from its resting place and drew it down to her side. The pepper spray went back into her bag, which she eased down onto the floor. Then she readied the shotgun with both hands, the business end leading the way as she moved away from the fireplace. She didn't have to wonder if it was loaded; Willy had kept it loaded at all times.

The cushions had been pulled from the sofa. Chairs overturned. The drawers of her gran's sideboard stood open haphazardly, the contents spilled onto the wide-plank wood floor. The cupboard doors and drawers were open as well, utensils and spices spewed over the countertop. Photographs and paintings that had once hung proudly on the walls lay on the floor, tossed aside like trash.

Fury whipped through Olivia. Her grandparents' beloved work. Willy had been the photographer, but it was Gran who had created amazing paintings of his work—paintings that had sold for thousands of dollars. Between their talents, they had amassed a small fortune. Though one would never know it based on his demeanor. Willy was never one to brag or to show off. His only remotely lavish purchase that Olivia was aware of was his Land Rover Defender—the vehicle he'd had since before she was born—and donations to charities focused on saving the planet. His and Gran's worldwide travels had convinced him the environment was on the verge of extinction.

Olivia paused before continuing into the hall. She tucked the butt of the shotgun firmly into her shoulder, rested her cheek against the stock and snugged her finger around the trigger. If someone was hiding in the house, he had better hope he could escape faster than she could lock in on him.

Unlikely.

With the curtains open on the windows, enough sunlight filtered in to prevent the rooms from being in shadow.

First room, her old room, was clear. Like the main living space, the room had been searched with no care for the value of anything or where it landed. Same in her grandparents' bedroom and the third bedroom—the one her parents had used. Her gran had insisted on keeping the room exactly as it was when Olivia's mother died. She hadn't been in the room in years. Once she'd surveyed the space, she closed the door and moved on. Even the single bathroom had been scoured for whatever the intruder had hoped to find.

Olivia relaxed the tiniest bit.

Weapon still held in a firing position, she moved back into the main living area and headed for the mudroom. Still no sound or abrupt movement. If anyone had still been in the house, she'd given him opportunity to flee by starting with the bedrooms. At this point, she felt fairly confident the house was empty. But she wasn't letting down her guard until she was certain.

The small mudroom was empty, but the back door was open.

Arms shaking from the extended tension, she lowered the shotgun. She started to reach for the door to close and lock it but stopped herself. There could be finger prints. She needed to call the police.

Olivia blinked, steadied herself. Whoever had ransacked the rest of the house had searched this room too.

She leaned against the shelves of canned goods and dug her cell phone from her pocket. Rather than tie up a 911 dispatcher, she called the sheriff's office directly. The woman who took Olivia's call assured her she would let the sheriff know and someone would be out shortly.

Deep breath. She tucked the phone into the hip pocket of her jeans and dared to close her eyes for a moment to gather herself. Willy was dead. Someone had come into his home and searched for something. But what?

Olivia opened her eyes and pushed away from the shelf-lined wall. She had no idea, but she damned well intended to find out. She marched over to the front door, her steps full of new purpose. There were a number of outbuildings, a barn and big old shed Willy had turned into a darkroom for himself and a studio for Gran. While she waited for the sheriff or one of his deputies, she should check those places too. What kind of person took advantage of a death to ransack a man's home? The question sent a new surge of outrage roaring through her.

Focus on what needs to be done.

Willy had taught Olivia how to search for lost things. How to take an area and divide it into a grid and cover those individual sections without missing a single square foot of the overall area. There were no footprints to be found. Apparently, it hadn't rained in several days. Moving on, she searched the barn first. The big old structure was basically untouched. The garden tools and tractor were just exactly as they were the last time Olivia had reason to go into the rambling space. The shed was a different story. The place had been turned upside down.

What in the world had the intruder been searching for?

Money? Willy certainly hadn't kept much money lying around the house, but even a small amount might seem like a lot to someone desperate enough to do this.

However, Olivia suspected the perpetrator had left utterly dissatisfied if the goal had been cash or items easily converted to cash.

The one thing she hadn't spotted so far was Willy's camera. Not just any camera either. It was a rare vintage Nikon. More important to Olivia than the monetary value was the sentimental value. The camera had been like an extension of Willy. Wherever he was, the Nikon was. He went absolutely nowhere without it. Though it was likely worth several thousand dollars, selling it would be a problem. The thief would need to find someone with a keen interest in photography to land anywhere near what the camera was worth. Otherwise, it would go for very little. She walked back to the house and propped the shotgun behind the front door. She stared at the mess and, despite her best efforts, cried again.

By the time an SUV bearing the sheriff's department logo arrived, Olivia had pulled herself together once more and gone through the house again in search of the camera. It was not there, which made sense since Willy would not have left the house without it. Why hadn't the Nikon been found with him? If he'd had it with him, and he most assuredly would have, then it had to be in the vicinity of where he had been found. Seemed like a very good question to ask the deputy climbing out of the SUV. It wasn't the sheriff, which was fine by her. She wasn't ready to see anyone who had been that close to Willy.

Olivia braced herself. So far she'd gotten through the search without falling completely apart, but she'd been on a mission. Adrenaline and anger had been fueling her. The anger had fizzled out at this point, and the adrenaline had faded. Her bravado was sinking fast.

Hold it together a little while longer.

As the deputy walked toward the porch, he removed his cap and gave her a nod. "Liv." When he reached the steps, he glanced down, gave his head a shake. "I am so sorry about Willy."

Maybe it was her mind's decision to zero in on the neatly pressed button-down shirt that seemed to barely contain broad shoulders and the faded jeans hugging long legs that threw her off. Or the baseball cap with the gold star emblazoned on it that he held in his hands—hands she knew as well as her own—that caused her to suddenly lose the ability to speak. No. It was none of those things. It was *him.*

Huck Monroe.

What was he doing here? Had he heard about Willy's death already? Had he driven all the way up from Miami? Wasn't he a sheriff's deputy there? Despite the circumstances, she almost laughed out loud. Huck Monroe had never visited. Not once that she was aware of in ten damned years. Why would he bother now?

"What're you doing here?" she demanded.

Her brain was playing tricks on her, obviously. She hadn't been able to read the identifying letters on the cap as it hung from his hands. But the Hamilton County SUV was sitting in the driveway, the lettering large and easily readable. Yet that made no sense. Huck had taken off for sun and sand and whatever else in south Florida that had attracted him forever ago.

He offered a sad smile. "I live here now." Hitched his head toward the SUV. "I'm a detective with the sheriff's department."

Wait. What? "When?" It was the only word she could force past her lips.

Why hadn't Willy told her about Huck coming back home? Maybe because she had made it clear she did not want to hear that name ever again.

She blinked away the memory of shouting those words at Willy.

What did it matter and why would she care? Particularly at the moment. The fissure in her heart widened. Her grandfather was dead.

Maybe she swayed the slightest bit, or her

face paled. Whatever the case, Huck reached for her.

"You okay?" His hand clamped around her arm to steady her.

No. She tugged away from his grasp. She couldn't do this. Not right now. "I need someone else." Her move to get away turned into more of a stumble back a couple of steps. The worry that clouded his face turned her confusion to renewed anger.

No. This was not acceptable.

"Why don't we go inside and have a seat?" he offered, ignoring her demand. "Then you can tell me what's going on?"

What she wanted was to call the sheriff's office and ask that they send someone else, but even in her current emotionally charged state she understood that would be petty and silly. She simply needed to pull herself together and get this done. When the words and images whirling in her head had calmed and her heart had stopped twisting, she could think more clearly. She had to make that happen sooner rather than later. This was not the time for childish behavior.

Deep breath. "Fine."

She turned and walked into the house. He followed.

"Wow." Huck gave a long, low whistle.

Yeah, she thought. Wow.

"Have you had a look around?" he asked as he surveyed the mess. "Noticed anything missing?"

"I looked around, yes. I can't find his Nikon." She rested her hands on her hips to prevent the shaking that had started there. What was wrong with her? Even her knees suddenly felt rubbery.

Shock. This had all been too much for a person who'd had no sleep in more than twenty-four hours and, now that she thought about it, hadn't eaten.

"His camera is missing?"

"I think so. At least, I haven't found it." She nodded, feeling overwhelmed. "I tried not to touch anything once I was beyond the front door." She glanced back in that direction. "Other than Willy's shotgun. I carried it with me through the house and when I checked the barn and shed."

"You were smart to be careful." He gave a nod. "We'll get our crime-scene investigators out here to check for prints."

The swell of emotions was back. Fierce and insistent, like a swarm of bees expelled from their colony and searching for a new hive. Another idea, one far more sinister leached into her soul. Her eyes didn't know where to land. Her heart was unsure of how to slow down and efficiently pump. She felt on the verge of collapse, and yet she wanted to run screaming through the woods.

This could not be happening.

"They said he fell." Her gaze settled on him... Huck—the boy she'd fallen in love with at fifteen. The boy with whom she'd thought she would be spending the rest of her life. The man who had decided not to wait for her. The man who had left and never looked back.

She sank into the closest chair. She was exhausted. The call from the sheriff had come at two yesterday afternoon. She had left work, rushed back to her townhouse, thrown a few things into a bag and hopped into her car. She had literally driven all night, stopping only for gas. Her brain was no longer functioning properly; otherwise, she would know exactly what to say and do next. She was generally far more collected and self-assured than this.

Willy was dead.

Gone forever.

She surveyed the chaos left behind in his home.

And someone had done this...it was no accident.

Huck was suddenly next to her, crouched

down and looking her directly in the eyes.
"The medical examiner found nothing to suggest foul play. Nothing at all suspicious." He
surveyed the carnage in the room. "But unless
you believe your grandfather made this mess
himself or we can find something more that's
missing, we need to determine if there's a connection between his fall and what we see here
that would suggest a different conclusion."

Was he proposing that someone had killed
Willy?

"This—" she waved her hand at the room
"—makes you think someone may have pushed
him?"

Who would do such a thing? For the most
part, Willy had been a hermit in his later years.
He and her gran traveled the world in the early
days, as much time on the road as at home.
At least until Olivia's mother reached school
age, and then they'd had to give up so much
traveling to raise their daughter. Not once had
her grandparents ever spoken of a single regret. They had loved this place. A lump swelled
in her throat. He was gone. The last member
of her family. Tears burned her eyes all over
again.

She blinked and glared at the man who

hadn't answered her question. "What are you saying?" she demanded.

"This," he said, "is the definition of suspicious circumstances."

Chapter Two

Huck Monroe kept an eye on Olivia. She looked ready to fall to pieces. She'd lost her grandfather, her last remaining family. Worse, now there was reason to believe—at least in Huck's opinion—foul play may have been involved.

The crime-scene unit had arrived an hour ago, but they were far from finished. Though the Ballard cabin wasn't very big, the old man had kept a lot of stuff. Huck wouldn't call him a hoarder, but he definitely wasn't one to let go of anything easily. Too many memories, he would always say. There were more photographs in the house than anything else. But then William Ballard had been a photographer with a long, much celebrated career and numerous prestigious awards.

Huck's gaze slid back to the swing hanging from that big old tree where Olivia had sequestered herself. The massive oak had always been her favorite. His too really. They'd climbed it enough times. Her grandfather had hung that swing when Olivia's mother was a child.

She looked so alone. His gut clenched. His first inclination was to comfort her, but they no longer had that kind of relationship. Ten years was a long time not to speak to someone, but Olivia hadn't forgiven him yet. He doubted she would have spoken to him today if not for the terrible circumstances.

She hadn't been home in months. Willy had told him she was home last Christmas. Oddly enough, Huck had almost driven over to see her. He'd moved back to Hamilton County earlier in the fall. Willy had been only too happy to have Huck back in the area. He'd welcomed him as if nothing bad had ever happened.

Obviously, he hadn't told Olivia about Huck's return. Probably hadn't wanted to deal with the backlash. Olivia didn't talk to or about Huck, Willy had explained. Never wanted to hear his name again. At least that was what she'd said the last time, according to Willy, that he'd mentioned Huck. She hated him for leaving. Refused to consider or even hear his reasons.

Huck walked back into the house. He couldn't keep standing on the porch staring at her, no matter that he wanted to. He'd repeatedly suggested she let him take her somewhere else—his place, a hotel, any place so she wouldn't have to watch this painful but necessary step. She had refused, of course.

He really couldn't blame her. She had every right to feel the way she did, even if he hadn't wanted to admit it a decade ago. Time had changed his mind, made him see his own mistakes in what happened. The truth was, he'd had no good reason for leaving. Other than the fact that she'd gone to Atlanta for college and seeing her only every other weekend had made him restless and more than a little jealous. He'd lasted more than a year, nearly two. Managed to get through the academy and start work as a sheriff's deputy. He'd been happy for a while, then he'd made a mistake he couldn't take back. He'd decided on a surprise visit to see her in Atlanta. Her schedule was so hectic they'd had to plan any visits. He'd known this well, but he'd gone anyway. The certainty that she would somehow outgrow him had planted deep roots in his psyche. Had made him doubt her.

Then he'd seen her with friends. Study friends, she always explained. Whenever she spent the whole weekend studying and other people were involved, she called them study friends. He'd seen her and those friends gathered around picnic tables in a park near the university. Huck had started toward the group, but then he'd noticed the guy who seemed particularly taken with Olivia.

His real mistake had been in not walking over to that picnic table and introducing himself. Instead, Huck had spent the entire weekend shadowing Olivia and her friends. The closeness, the comradery he'd seen had been like a flash from the future. He would never be like those people. He hadn't gone to college, had no plans to. He didn't drive a sports car or wear the latest fashions.

He just didn't fit in with the life he saw happening for Olivia. The last thing he wanted to do was hold her back. He had remembered vividly all the conversations about traveling the world and exploring the possibilities out there. By twenty-one, he had realized his possibilities were far more limited than hers.

He hadn't wanted Olivia to ever feel in any way limited. So he'd left. Taken a job as a deputy in Miami-Dade County. Olivia would be better off without having to worry about him. He'd left without a word to her or to her grandfather.

She hadn't forgiven him.

He'd made a mistake.

He considered the painting of Olivia one of the techs was processing. It had hung over the fireplace, just above that shotgun rack, for as long as Huck could remember. Incredibly, she was even more beautiful now than she was as a young girl and that was saying something. Never married. Traveled the world. Worked in places he'd never even dreamed of visiting. Then a year ago, she'd taken a more permanent position in Montana. Willy figured she had decided it was time to settle down.

Huck wondered if there was someone. He shook his head. None of his business.

He'd given up that right better than ten years ago.

Funny, when he was near her, it felt like only yesterday that they had last kissed. That her fingers had caressed his jaw and her long, silky hair had whispered against his skin.

He shook off the thoughts and focused on the work. Something had gone down in this house, perhaps before Willy went over that cliff. Huck intended to find the truth. He owed the man. Not only because he had forgiven Huck and welcomed him back as if he'd never left, but because he had always treated Huck like family. Huck would not fail him now.

He wouldn't fail Olivia either.

A walk through the house gave him a good

idea of how much more time was needed, then he headed outside to update Olivia. She should decide where she intended to stay for the night. He didn't see any reason she couldn't return to the house in the morning, but that wasn't happening tonight.

As he approached, her head came up. "Have they found anything?"

He hadn't thought about it until that moment, but she hadn't said his name. Not once in the past couple of hours had she called him Huck. Clearly, she still hated him. It wasn't like she didn't have every right to.

"We won't know until the analysis is complete. In any home, there are lots of prints. Screening the ones that should be there from the ones that shouldn't takes time. So far, nothing that shouldn't be here has been found."

She nodded, opened her mouth to say something and then closed it.

"This is a really tough time for you," he said, softening his voice despite the tension humming inside him. "To get this kind of news and then come home to a scene like this one. It's hard. As difficult as it is, the best thing you can do is get a good night's sleep and come back in the morning. You'll see things more clearly then."

Olivia stared at him, her dark eyes digging

deep into him, making him want to hug the hell out of her. He imagined she wouldn't be too happy if he tried.

"You're right." She looked away. "I should go to a hotel and get some sleep." She stood, leaving the old wooden swing to sway listlessly in the air. "I'll be able to digest all this better tomorrow."

An urgency plowed through him. The strangest thought that maybe if he let her get away, he wouldn't see her again for another ten years accompanied the sensation.

"Look," he said, his voice rough, "I know this might sound a little crazy, but I moved into the old homeplace. It's a big house. There's plenty of room, and I'll probably be here for most of the night, so you'd have the place to yourself."

She stared at him in something that resembled confusion or astonishment.

Rather than give her the chance to consider what he was saying, he dug out his keys, pulled the one for the house free and thrust it at her. "Go. You'll be safe there."

Then he managed a half smile, turned and headed back into the house. She didn't call after him. Didn't tell him to go to hell and fling his key at him. When he reached the front door of the cabin and dared to look back, she had walked to her car and climbed in. Relief washed over him. He watched until she was gone. It was the least he could do. Before he could go inside another vehicle arrived. Sheriff Arnold Decker himself.

Huck walked down the steps and headed toward his boss. Decker had turned the big seven-oh last year, but he had no plans to retire anytime soon. The citizens of Hamilton County loved the guy. He was a good man. A damned good sheriff. He'd been voted in by a landslide after the county's beloved Tarrence Norwood's ill health had forced him to retire.

"Monroe." Decker nodded. "What've we got here?"

The sheriff was far too busy to show up at every crime scene, especially one that hadn't been confirmed as of yet. But William Ballard wasn't just any victim. Back in the day, he had been one of Chattanooga's biggest and most beloved celebrities. Fact was, he and Decker had spent plenty of time fishing together. The two had been good friends for as long as Huck could recall.

"Olivia came home and found the house and shed a wreck."

Decker would know the shed wasn't just some place to store tools. It was Willy's darkroom and workplace. The space where award-winning photos had been developed. His wife's art studio was in there as well. She and Willy had turned that old building into an artist's work retreat before sheds were in for that sort of thing.

Decker settled his hands on his hips. "The ME's report said he fell." He shrugged. "An accident. No suspicious circumstances."

Huck nodded. "But the house and shed suggest a different story."

Decker swore, shook his head. "Let's have a look."

Chattanooga and the surrounding area might be Tennessee's fourth largest metropolitan area, but communities like Sunset Cove gave the area a small-town atmosphere where folks knew their neighbors. Huck had kicked himself repeatedly for ever leaving. He'd given up on Olivia and that had been the biggest mistake of all. Even Willy had worried that it might be too late to ever repair the damage. God knows they had discussed it many times.

Willy was gone now. Olivia had no reason to ever come back after this.

Huck's gut clenched with despair. Maybe it was too late, but damn it, when he'd seen her standing on her grandfather's porch, he'd felt like there might still be hope. Or maybe that had been wishful thinking. But he couldn't let her leave again without trying, could he?

Focus, pal.

Decker surveyed the chaos. "What the hell?" He shook his head, then turned to Huck. "You could be right," he admitted, "but we could also just be looking at someone who heard about his death and decided to capitalize on the situation. There's some pretty desperate folks out there with the state of the world these days."

Huck nodded. "I considered that too. But then I noticed the things that hadn't been taken. Mrs. Ballard's jewelry is still in the bedroom. Some of it looks pretty valuable. There's a small gold coin collection and various household goods that could be easily sold or traded for drugs." He shrugged. "So far, I haven't found a thing that's missing other than his camera. Olivia noticed it first. Unless it was found with his body, and I just haven't heard, it's gone."

Decker blew out a big breath. "Well, hell." His fierce gaze settled on Huck. "I want you to get to the bottom of this, Monroe. Willy was more than just a friend. If someone did this to him, I want to know."

"Yes, sir." He was preaching to the choir. Nobody in this county cared more about William Ballard than Huck.

"You let me know if you need anything," Decker went on, "and take care of Willy's granddaughter. He'd want us to make sure she's okay." He shook his head. "If she'd told me when she was arriving, I would have gone to the ME's office with her. Damn it."

Huck understood. He would have done the same. If he hadn't been in Nashville for that deposition, he would have been here anyway. But he hadn't heard the news until this morning. He'd wanted to call Olivia, but he didn't have her new cell number. She likely didn't want him to have it.

"You don't need to worry about Olivia, sir," Huck promised his boss. "I'll take care of her."

Huck intended to do everything in his power to make sure Olivia had whatever she needed for however long she was in town. She would be Huck's top priority. Maybe in the process of getting through this tragedy there was some way he could convince her to forgive him. And whoever did this to Willy, assuming it wasn't an accident, had better hope someone else found him before Huck.

Twilight Trail, 7:00 p.m.

OLIVIA SAT IN her car staring up at the house for a long time before she even attempted to talk herself into climbing out.

This farmhouse had been her second home

growing up. Huck's parents had been like the aunt and uncle she had never had. Willy and her gran were both only children, and her mom had been their only child.

She sank deeper into her seat. How sadly ironic that both her parents were only children. Her father had been a drifter until he landed in Nashville and met Laura Ballard during her freshman year at Vandy. She'd stolen his heart, he'd claimed. But after only a few short years, he'd disappeared. Then, Laura had died. In the span of one year Olivia had lost both her father and her mother.

For as far back as her memory went, no one ever talked about her father. As Olivia had gotten older, her gran had told her the few things she knew about him. Only child, drifter, etcetera. Huck had asked his parents about her dad, and they'd told her some things like the part about her mother having stolen his heart and how the two of them were away for weeks at a time even after Olivia was born. Her father's work, Gran had explained.

Olivia looked exactly like her mother. Same dark hair and eyes. Same everything, really. Looking at a photograph of her mother was like looking in the mirror. There were only a few photos of her father. He'd had sandy blond hair and blue eyes.

Like Huck.

Olivia closed her eyes to slow the whirlwind of thoughts and emotions. Huck had left her the same way her father had left her mother.

"Enough." She opened the car door and forced her feet on the ground and pushed herself into an upright position. It wasn't until she turned back for her overnight bag that she realized she'd left her purse at the cabin. Whatever. She was too tired to care. Huck would bring it. Maybe. They had exchanged cell phone numbers before she left. Apparently, Willy had done as she'd asked and never given him her newest number. She reached into the back and grabbed her overnight bag, then shoved the car door shut. Forcing one foot in front of the other, she walked to the house.

Unlike the cabin, Huck's family home stood two stories, with a basement and a huge attic. They'd explored every square inch of that attic as well as the basement. From ghost-hunter clubs to detective partnerships, they had played every imaginable game. Huck was only a year older than her, so they'd had a tremendous amount in common. If she told the truth, she would admit she'd loved him since they were kids. That love had just blossomed into something different as they grew older.

"Fool," she griped at herself for going down that road.

She climbed the steps. Couldn't help smiling at the pair of rockers that still sat on the porch. It seemed to Olivia that on hot summer evenings Huck's parents could always be found rocking on this porch. His dad had died suddenly late last year, and only a few months later his mom had moved to Knoxville to live with her older sister, who was also a widow. Didn't take much imagination to recognize she wouldn't have wanted to stay in this big old house alone. She probably hadn't expected Huck would ever come home. Olivia was shocked still that he'd decided to do so *after* his mother left.

Willy had made comments about folks in Sunset Cove, including Huck, even when Olivia hadn't wanted to know, particularly about Huck. She had been well aware Willy had always hoped she and Huck would find a way to work things out. Even after ten years, he'd held onto that foolish optimism.

Olivia hadn't had the heart to tell him that was never, ever going to happen.

She unlocked and opened the door. The familiar scents filled her senses. The aftershave Huck had always worn lingered in the air. How, in a house this large, could she smell *him* first and foremost? And why hadn't he started using something else? She didn't want to smell that scent.

Just stop.

Her grandfather was dead…the only person in this world who was biologically part of her. She was weak right now. Shaken by the idea that someone may have hurt him. Of course, she couldn't be expected to maintain her usual defenses. She was only human after all.

She closed the door, locked it and decided she needed a shower. Desperately.

She was almost to the stairs when a framed photo on the hall table stopped her.

Sam. Samson, the big old sweet Labrador that held a place in her fondest memories.

She dropped her bag. Picked up the frame and touched the image of the black dog.

He'd died the year after Huck had moved to Miami. He'd been seventeen at the time. This dog had been on a multitude of camping trips with Olivia and Huck. She'd never been able to have a dog of her own because this sweet animal had ruined her for any other pet.

She held the photograph to her chest and cried. Couldn't stop the tears. She collapsed onto the bottom step of the staircase. She cried for Willy and how she missed him so desperately. She cried for all the things that should have been and never would be. Mostly, she cried because she felt hollow and lost... adrift.

When she had cried herself out, she struggled to her feet. She steadied herself and placed the photograph back on the table. She remembered vividly how after her grandmother had died, she'd suffered with sudden crying bouts for months. She expected it would be the same this time.

She trudged up the stairs. Passed the bedroom that had belonged to Huck's parents and the one that had been—probably still was—his. She went to the room that had been a guest room for as long as she could remember and plunked her bag on the bed. She took out the nightshirt she'd brought and clean underwear. Then she made her way to the hall bathroom.

Blindly, she retrieved a towel from the shelf and climbed into the shower. It wasn't until the hot water had filled the cubical with steam that more of the scents she couldn't bear closed in on her. The soap she had smelled on his skin even though he'd barely touched her today. The shampoo he used. Emotion engulfed her once more, and she sank into it, embraced it. As painful as it was, at least it was something real.

She needed something, anything, to cling to right now.

Chapter Three

Olivia brushed her hair and pulled it into a ponytail to get it out of the way. This was her preferred hairstyle when in the field. Today it was about not having the strength to care. She stared at her reflection in the hazy mirror over the antique dresser. In time, the hurt would pass on to a more manageable level. She could do this. She was strong.

She closed her eyes and drew in a deep breath. Huck had been up for a while. First thing, when he got up, she'd heard him walk down the hall and stand outside her door. He hadn't knocked or said anything. She supposed he'd considered one or the other but changed his mind.

As much as she appreciated his generosity, she was glad he'd gone downstairs.

Going downstairs was something she had waffled back and forth about since the moment she woke up. Doing so meant facing him…on his home turf. It wasn't that she didn't feel completely at home here. She did. She had played in this house. Had dinners in that kitchen. Romped in the yard…had her first kiss in his bedroom at the ripe old age of thirteen.

She shook her head. The kiss had startled them both. He hadn't initiated it any more than she had, it just happened. They were listening to music and suddenly their faces were coming together. It hadn't happened again for a very long time. But they had held hands a lot after that. Running through the woods. Walking along the sidewalk in town. Watching movies. It was like they were connected and there was no way to separate one from the other. Her every thought and plan started and ended with him. What would Huck think? Do? When would he be over? What were they going to do today? When would they kiss again?

When she'd left for college, she hadn't once considered there would ever be life without Huck. They would be together forever just like they always had been.

Except they hadn't.

Olivia forced her head out of the past and grabbed her cell. She needed to charge it before heading out for the day. There was a lot to do, and she was woefully unprepared even after a good ten hours of sleep.

Steeling herself, she left the refuge of the borrowed room. The smell of burning toast accompanied the sound of swearing as she descended the stairs. Her lips lifted in a little smile. The idea that his morning didn't appear to be going so well helped her to relax just the tiniest bit. Maybe she wasn't the only one feeling utterly awkward.

She paused at the kitchen door and watched for a moment. He popped two slices of bread into the toaster and leaned down to adjust the browning control. On the stove, steam rose from a frying pan. Eggs more than a little overdone, she decided based on the odor wafting from that direction. Beyond those unpleasant scents was the smell of coffee. Now that mustered her attention.

Olivia moved into the room. "Good morning."

Huck straightened and turned to face her. "I hope I didn't wake you with all my…" He waved a hand at the mess he'd made. "I've never been much of a cook. Mom never let me near the kitchen, and in Miami it was too easy to hit a drive-through to bother with honing any chef skills." He shut off the stove eye and considered the eggs. "We should probably do that today in fact."

"It's okay. I'm not really hungry." She glanced toward the sink. The coffeepot still stood next to that big old farmhouse-style sink tucked beneath a double window. Huck's mom had always said staring out that window with her cup of coffee each morning before anyone else was up was one of her favorite parts of the day. "Coffee, I need desperately."

He grinned. "Good thing I do that quite well."

He walked to the counter, grabbed a mug he'd already placed there and poured the brew. "Black, right?" He turned, offered the steaming mug to her.

"Right." She crossed the room, accepted the warm cup. "Thanks."

He swiped at his blue T-shirt as if suddenly feeling underdressed. "I brought your handbag from the cabin. It's on the sofa."

"Great. Thank you. I need my charger."

He held out a hand. "Give me your phone, and I'll put it on my charger." He hitched his head toward the door. Sure enough, one of those handy charging stations sat on the counter by the back door. "I put mine on the charger every evening when I come home."

She slid her phone from her hip pocket and placed it in his broad hand. "Thanks."

Olivia pulled out a chair at the table and took

a seat. After he'd put her phone on the charger, he poured himself a cup of coffee and joined her. His every move—the way he'd reached toward her, the way he turned, even the way he sat down—were all as familiar to her as breathing. She knew him as well as she knew herself, and yet after ten years apart, they were strangers now.

Some things, she supposed, were too deeply engrained to be erased even by time.

She was pretty sure she recognized the faded blue tee too. Vintage for sure. All the way back to when they were teenagers and in love with classic rock. But the logo wasn't why she remembered the tee. It brought out the perfect blue in his eyes. Made her want to lean closer to make sure she wasn't imagining such a pale, pale blue color. People he met always commented on the unusual color of his eyes. The body-hugging jeans were, of course, classic Huck.

How was it that she hadn't thought of him in years and suddenly she was here, with him, and her entire being felt as if she had missed him desperately every minute of every day for more than a decade? Felt as if the part of her that had been missing was suddenly right in front of her.

She was emotional, she told herself. Losing Willy had broken her defenses. Made her weaker than she'd expected. Made her frantic for human connection.

She sipped her coffee and somehow managed to keep the emotions that attempted to crowd into her chest under some facsimile of control.

Huck looked up from the cup he'd been staring into. Maybe he was struggling with the situation as well. "It's good to see you, Liv, no matter that I'm sorry as hell for the reason you're here. You know I loved Willy."

She did know. Just like that, here came those damned tears again, burning her eyes. She blinked at them, attempted a smile. "I know." She swallowed at the lump clogging her throat. "We talked several times every week." Her smile was boosted at the memory of his voice. "He was still taking photos even at seventy-two. He detailed his every foray on the trails he knew I loved so much. It was almost like I was still here."

If she walked those trails now, she wouldn't be surprised at nature's changes. He'd kept her updated on every single detail. Olivia had decided that he had missed his second calling by not writing a book or two. His ability to describe the landscape and capture its full beauty in words as well as on film had been inspiring.

"The man was healthy, strong. Went hiking every day." Huck shook his head. "He knew those trails better than anyone."

Images from the house and shed populated her brain like files on an awakening computer screen. "I can't believe he would have gotten too close and fallen." She squeezed her eyes shut and shook her head. "He was too careful to make that kind of mistake." She took a deep breath, opened her eyes once more. "I realize anyone can make a mistake—stumble—I get that…but Willy was well versed in all the ways to recapture one's balance. To handle the unexpected."

"That's what I told the sheriff."

"He and Willy were friends," Olivia said aloud, remembering all those fishing trips and all those tales of adventures as young men. "What does he think?"

Huck shrugged. "He believes the case could go either way. Willy was old, like him, he said. Sometimes you lose your balance unexpectedly."

The ravages of age affected everyone, but Willy would have borne that in mind. He hadn't been fool enough to believe otherwise. "So, he believes it was an accident?"

"He did," Huck admitted, "until he saw the

cabin. He said I should do whatever it takes to determine what happened either way."

Olivia studied him a moment. The tension in his shoulders. The restlessness in his hands as he turned the mug around and around. "What do you think happened?" she asked, needing to know for sure she wasn't in this alone.

His eyes connected with hers, the weight of worry heavy. "I don't know, but I'm leaning toward the idea that it was not an accident, and I damned sure intend to find the answer one way or another."

Fighting a renewed burst of emotion, she said, "Willy didn't have any enemies that I know of."

Huck shook his head. "No way. Everybody loved him."

"Except whoever pushed him." The words twisted in her gut like barbed wire.

Their gazes collided again. "We'll figure this out."

"I want to go there." She drew in a deep breath. "To Sunset Rock. I need to see it." She needed to breathe the air...to feel what he'd felt in those final moments. Her heart thudded harder with the weight of pain.

Huck nodded. "I'll take you."

Sunset Rock, 10:30 a.m.

HUCK INSISTED THEY grab something to eat on the way. Olivia had been certain she couldn't possibly eat, but when he'd come out of the diner with that bag of buttered biscuits with bacon, she'd eaten.

To reach their destination, they had parked at Point Park and proceeded on foot along the trail. Willy would have done it that way. He'd done it thousands of times. So had Olivia. So had Huck. It was the most inspirational route. Besides, Huck had already said his Defender had been parked there. The sheriff had driven the vehicle back to the house after his body was recovered.

This place was nothing short of awe-inspiring. The vast, long mountain ridge cut through Alabama, Georgia and Tennessee, rising far above the Cumberland Plateau. Hikers, trail runners and climbers loved it. The trails in the area never got old, not even to the folks who had lived here their whole lives. She was lucky to have grown up in the Lookout Mountain area. Considering the stunning views, the place was aptly named. Oh, and the caves. So many caves. As a kid, Olivia had tagged along on many cave explorations with Willy. When they were old enough, she and Huck had explored plenty on their own as well.

Willy had only one rule about her and Huck venturing into this beautiful yet dangerous terrain: always provide someone a thorough plan for your trip before you leave. The exact route, departure time and anticipated return time. It was the golden rule, particularly for those hiking alone.

Had Willy told anyone where he was going that last day? Or had his number one rule been only for others?

Nearly two miles from where they parked, they reached Sunset Rock. High above the Tennessee River and the world below. The sheer drops from Sunset Rock were sudden and steep. It was no place to be distracted. The unprotected drops were far too dangerous not to use extreme caution no matter how often you visited.

And no matter the danger…no matter the hurt this place now wielded for her, Olivia lost her breath as she took it in.

"It doesn't matter how many times you see it," Huck said, reading her mind, "it's beautiful in a way that's difficult to explain."

"This is the last thing Willy saw." The idea gave her a sense of peace and at the same time stabbed deep into her chest.

They stood there for a very long time, experiencing the solitude, soaking up the beauty. They hadn't met a soul on the way up or when they arrived, so they were completely alone in this vast, stunning terrain. The silence felt right. For Willy, she decided. This was the perfect place to remember him. No matter where his body was, his soul would be flying here.

After a time, Huck said, "Do you remember what we used to do sometimes?"

She turned to stare up at him, wondering if he meant the same thing she had just recalled. Then he reached for her hand, and she knew he did.

"Just close your eyes," he said softly as his fingers curled around hers.

Olivia closed her eyes. She didn't have to look to know Huck did the same.

Back when they were together…before… they would come up here, ease as close to the edge as they dared, and then stand very still with their eyes closed. It was like floating high above all else…like being the only people on earth with unseen forces drawing them closer and closer.

When she couldn't bear the silence or the pull of him any longer, she opened her eyes and tugged free of his hold. His eyes opened, the pain there not unlike her own.

"I want to see where they found him."

He nodded. "Okay."

The trek down was quiet, somber. Olivia drifted into a kind of numbness she hoped would get her through the part that came next.

When Huck led her off the visible path, there was no crime-scene tape, no evidence markers. But when he stopped, she recognized the place. There was evidence of disturbance amid the plant life. Grasses smashed by the landing. Trampled by rescuers. Rocks pushed aside. Blood.

Olivia blinked. Stared at the stain on one fairly large boulder.

The point of impact.

Her stomach dropped, and she felt sick.

"Are you sure about this?" Huck was next to her, his hand on her arm.

With effort, Olivia pushed the frailer emotions aside. "They didn't find his camera."

If it wasn't at the house or in the shed, it had to be here. She had checked in the Defender and it hadn't been there either.

Unless…someone took it.

"I doubt the rescue crew would have known to look for it," Huck offered.

Valid point. Olivia looked up, her eyes searching for the most likely place where he would have gone over the edge. Her guts tied into knots, but she had to do this. It was too important. If someone caused Willy's death, he couldn't be permitted to get away with it.

"Let's spread out, but be careful." Huck studied her a long moment. "I'm guessing you haven't done this in a while."

He was likely assuming as much based on the sneakers she wore. Her hiking boots were back in Montana, and he was right; she hadn't done this in a while. Her promotion to project manager had sentenced her to more time in the office.

"I'm good," she said rather than admit the truth in his words.

Beyond the well-traveled trail, the brush was thick. The terrain rocky. Treacherous in places. But she kept going. Creating a grid of sorts around the point of impact.

She shuddered each time the words echoed through her brain. Somehow the more technical term wasn't as awful as "the place where he died."

Willy was dead.

Hurt made breathing difficult, but she kept going. She prowled through the greenery, poked around between the rocks. Memories from the hundreds if not thousands of journeys she and Huck had made along these trails kept intruding on her thoughts. There was a cave, more a narrow crevice in the rocks upon first glance, somewhere around here. She and Huck had tucked themselves away there so many times. Reading. Talking about the future. Stealing kisses.

As if her thoughts had led her there, she found that secret place. Probably not really secret but not easily seen or found. She slipped beyond the crevice and into the wider part of the space created by the rock walls that had split apart eons ago. Digging out her cell, she used the flashlight app to study the walls. Found what she was looking for and traced her fingers over the slight indentions in the rock. Huck had spent hours slowly chiseling their initials into the rock.

"A million years ago," she murmured.

She leaned her head against the cool rock. All those years ago, who would have thought this was where they would be now. Torn apart. Her heart battered. Maybe his too. Willy gone.

Olivia closed her eyes and breathed through the pain. Life would never be the same. She thought of all the things she wished she had said to Willy the last time they had talked just three days ago. Had she told him she loved him? That she missed him? That she wished she had stayed closer all these years?

It was sadly true. So many times in the past

decade she had considered that she'd made a mistake traveling the world with her work rather than being close to home. Egypt. Mexico. Peru. Chile. Greece. Had those weeks and months spent at archaeological sites been worth it?

She had thought so at the time. Willy had loved hearing all about it. He'd told her about showing off the pictures she shared with him. She'd sent him endless treasures from her adventures.

But none of those were the same as spending time with him.

"I wondered where you'd gotten off to."

Huck's voice had her opening her eyes. His cell phone light was pointed at the ground but provided enough illumination for her to see him.

Unlike when they were kids and the space was enough to comfortably accommodate the two of them, his broad shoulders required that he turn slightly to fit now. The air in the space felt suddenly lacking. Not nearly enough. His scent…his presence filled it up. Closed in around her.

"I'd forgotten about this place." She looked around, anywhere but at him.

"I come here sometimes."

She frowned. Confused. Couldn't *not* look at him then. "You do?"

"Sure. We spent so much time here it feels like a place I don't want to forget."

The way she had.

"Why?" she asked.

"Why what?"

It was too dark to see his face well enough for her to read his expression, but the confusion was quite clear in his voice.

Maybe it was the darkness or this place that gave her the courage to delve into the until now forbidden subject. "Why did you come back to Sunset Cove?"

He didn't answer for a while. Maybe a whole minute.

"Mom was moving to her sister's. Aunt Gloria couldn't stay home without help, and there was no one else." He shrugged. Olivia didn't so much see the move as hear his shoulders scrape the rock. "To tell you the truth, I think she hadn't been happy in the house since Dad died."

"I'm sorry," Olivia said, suddenly realizing that she owed him an apology for not attending his father's funeral. "I was in Peru when your father died. Communications at the dig site were minimal. I didn't get the word that he'd died until a week later."

"Willy told me."

"He was like my second father," she admitted. "I loved him."

The silence went on for too long. She'd said more than she should have.

"Anyway," Huck said abruptly. "Mom was ready for a change, but she didn't want to abandon the place. She said I should take the place and make it my own. So that's what I did."

"That was very noble of you." She didn't believe for a moment he'd left his life in Miami behind and come back here just because someone needed to take care of the house. Or maybe it was just easier to believe that since she had stayed gone too.

"Not really," he said. "I was ready to come home. I'd been considering moving back for a while when she asked."

The idea that Olivia had been struggling with the same feelings hit too close. This was too much. Way too much.

"Do you mind? I'm feeling a little claustrophobic?"

Without a word, he slipped away. For a moment she waited in the near darkness, her heart hammering at having abruptly lost the closeness.

Big breath. Don't think about it.

Olivia followed the path he'd taken. Once

they were back on the trail, he said, "I don't think we're going to find his camera. Either he didn't bring it with him, or someone took it."

Like his killer.

Deep inside, Olivia shuddered. "He never went anywhere without it. You know that."

"Yeah." He surveyed the landscape. "I do."

Which left only one option.

Someone took it. After viewing the scene, Olivia couldn't see how the camera would have survived the fall. The film with whatever pics he'd taken may have been salvageable but not the camera. Which made the idea that someone had taken it even more ludicrous.

Unless he took it before Willy fell. The scenario played out in her head. Willy trying to hang on to the camera…losing his hold…falling…

Olivia forced the images away.

The possibility brought up another question: Was there something on the camera that mattered to the person who took it? Something important enough to kill for?

Uneasiness slid through Olivia. "Do you think he may have taken a photo of something or someone that made him a target?"

"I guess it's possible." Huck glanced at her. "You're thinking someone just passing through? Maybe Willy came upon some sort of trouble?"

Olivia didn't respond right away. She kept walking, heading back. Huck did the same. "It could happen."

"It could. Wrong place, wrong time sort of thing."

"Or maybe someone he knew from his traveling days. Someone who wanted money or whatever from him?"

"Had he mentioned having any visitors?"

Olivia shook her head. "But he did seem distracted the last time we talked."

"When was that?"

"Sunday. We talked that morning." Olivia considered the conversation. "It was shorter than usual. Willy said he had a lot to do." Looking back, his rush to get off the phone had seemed more urgent than she'd realized at the time. Or perhaps his death only made it seem so.

"What about his cell phone?" Olivia had only just thought of the device. Willy generally took his cell with him. To him, it wasn't as essential as his camera, but over time he had come to see that it was immensely handy.

"It should be in his vehicle," Huck said. "Sheriff Decker drove the Defender back to the house. I'm sure he would have left it in the vehicle as long as it was found and not needed for evidence."

"It could be evidence," Olivia argued. She didn't remember seeing it when she'd looked for the camera but, honestly, she hadn't even thought about the phone.

"Now that we have suspicious circumstances," Huck confirmed, "that's correct, and I've ordered his cell phone records, which will show us all calls or messages, even those that may have been erased from his cell. So if we don't find it, we can still determine who he was in contact with."

"We should check the Defender and see if it's there," Olivia said, needing to see it. To know something now.

"We'll do that first, then I think we should go through the house more thoroughly," Huck suggested. "This is my case, and I intend to focus solely on it until we figure this out. Decker said I should take all the time I need."

Olivia paused. "Thank you. I'm sure you could have passed off the case, but I appreciate you doing this personally, Huck."

Her breath caught. She hadn't said his name out loud in so, so long. It felt foreign and yet somehow normal…natural. She had known this man her whole life…knew every part of him by heart just as he knew every part of her. Strangely, for once it didn't hurt to say it.

He gave a curt nod and kept walking.

By the time they reached the parking lot, Olivia decided she had overstepped. The thick silence had been evidence enough. Although she didn't see how he had a right to be put off by anything she might feel or say. After all, he was the one to leave and start a new life. Given his leaving and staying gone so long, it was reasonable for her to feel his offer of help was unexpected. Over the top even. She would not feel guilty for saying what needed to be said.

By the time they had reached his SUV, she decided to just be honest. If they were going to work together to find the truth about what happened to Willy, honesty was important. All this tension and subterfuge would just be in the way.

Being the gentleman his daddy had taught him to be, Huck opened the passenger-side door for her.

Olivia hesitated before climbing in. "Look, all I was trying to say back there is that, after all this time, I do appreciate your decision to go the extra mile."

He turned to her, anger or maybe frustration radiating from him. "First," he said tightly, "Willy was like family to me. I would do anything to help. Second…" He stalled, took a breath. "It's my job."

Olivia felt oddly calm. Maybe it was the calm before the storm, but she was grateful for the ability to speak evenly. "You're right. Still, it's above and beyond. You were gone a long time. Never reached out. Didn't drop by if you ever visited your folks. I would understand if you'd chosen to pass."

He held up both hands. "Wait. You're saying my help is unexpected because *I* left ten years ago?"

Her own anger and frustration stirred. "That's right."

"You left first."

The three words were heavy with accusation.

Olivia's mouth dropped open. "I went to school. I—" she slapped her chest "—was coming back when I graduated."

He bit his lips together so hard she wondered how his teeth didn't crack. When she would have launched her next barb, he spoke again, "I don't know where you got your information, but I visited Willy whenever I was in town. Called him at least once every month."

His words stunned her. Seriously? Why would Willy not have told her that part?

Because you didn't want to hear anything about Huck.

"I called you." The words were out before

she could recall them. Humiliation swaddled her, suffocating and frustrating. But she'd said it. She couldn't unsay it any more than he could unhear it. "Over and over. In the beginning, I mean. Left messages for you with your parents. You never once called back."

"We should get going." He reached for the SUV door.

She glared at him. And there it was. The truth of the matter. He'd left, and even when she called, leaving countless messages for him to please, please call her back…he hadn't.

He just left without looking back.

Olivia settled into the passenger seat and buckled her seat belt. She would take his help if it meant finding out what happened to Willy.

But she would never, ever forgive him.

Chapter Four

Huck parked behind Olivia's car. Putting aside their personal issues, they had agreed that the next step was to more thoroughly search the cabin and the shed. He'd taken her back to his house to get her car and overnight bag. She'd insisted. He had a feeling that decision had something to do with not wanting to be committed to going back to his place at the end of the day.

Nothing he could do about that. She was a grown damned woman. He watched her climb out of her car and walk to the porch. He'd thought she was the prettiest girl he'd ever seen when they were kids, but that didn't begin to describe her now.

As angry as she made him, she was a beautiful woman. Just looking at her…listening to her voice undid him.

Get your head on straight, man.

He climbed out of his vehicle and headed toward the house. He stopped at the Defender and checked for Willy's cell phone. It wasn't in the vehicle. Good thing he'd ordered his phone records. As he headed inside, he considered how much easier it might be if he just told her the reason he'd taken off all those years ago. But it wouldn't change anything. The fact was he'd eventually realized that he'd made a mistake, but by then there was no turning back. Why tell her what an idiot he'd been? How his immaturity and insecurity had ruined their lives? That his ego disguised as concern for her had been leading him? It wouldn't change one damned thing.

What was done was done.

No looking back. That motto had helped him survive losing her.

Forward—he had to keep pushing forward or lose his sanity altogether.

The crime-scene investigators were finished with the property, so he and Liv were free to do as they pleased. Considering how much stuff Willy had, going through it all thoroughly would take some time.

His gaze landed on Olivia, who stood in the middle of the living room. Huck just hoped they got through the journey without her hat-ing him even more. He wasn't sure he could survive another stab to the heart.

She turned to face him, and the air rushed out of his lungs. His hopes died a sudden death. He would not survive this either way.

"I appreciate you taking me to…where it happened." She drew back her shoulders, lifted her chin. "But I've got this part from here."

While he recovered from her unexpected statement, she surveyed the room and went on, "I mean here—in the house. I've got this. I'm sure you have plenty of police work to do on the case without hanging around with me."

"There could be evidence *here*," he said, finding his voice and a reasonable comeback.

"If I discover any evidence, I'll call you." She walked past him and to the door, opened it. "Thanks again."

He felt the knife slice deep between his ribs. He wanted to shake her and demand to know why it had to be this way. Couldn't they at least be friends? Get along like two people who had known each other their whole lives minus all the emotional stuff?

But he said none of those things. He made his way to the door. Should have walked on out. Shouldn't have paused even for a second. But, apparently, he wasn't that smart.

He stared down his shoulder at her. "It doesn't have to be this way."

She looked up at him, her expression firm, her lips tight. "*This* is the way it is."

Maybe it was the fire in her eyes—the absolute blazing determination in her voice—but he felt the burn on his back when he walked out all the way to his SUV.

He swung open the driver-side door and slid behind the wheel, his frustrated gaze still on that damned door. She stood there, watching him. She wanted to ensure he left. Wanted to watch him go.

On autopilot, he started the engine, shifted into Reverse and peeled away without taking his eyes off her. He could watch too, by God.

He slammed on the brakes, hit Drive and roared away.

Yeah, he was a fool. He slowed his speed. Pounded the steering wheel with the heel of his hand. He was thirty-one damned years old, and he'd just acted like a rebellious teenager.

Olivia Ballard was the one person in this world who could turn him inside out that way. Make him want to tear something apart…like the life he'd spent a decade building—the one without her.

His chest tightened to the point he could scarcely breathe. Ten years was a long time but not nearly long enough to forget her. He'd kept hoping someday she would hunt him down and tell him she'd never stopped loving him. That he'd made a mistake when he left and she was tired of waiting for him to admit it. But that was a fantasy that only worked in his dreams.

The warning that he'd failed to put on his seatbelt finally punctured the haze of anger and frustration blurring his good sense. He slowed, yanked the belt across his lap and snapped the buckle.

"Idiot," he growled.

His cell vibrated, and he dragged it from his pocket. *Sheriff* flashed on the screen. He hit Accept. "Monroe."

"Huck, I've asked the medical examiner to have a second look at Willy. He says he can do it today and release the body tomorrow. Pass that on to Olivia, would you?"

"Yes, sir." The idea of having to go back and talk to her had his throat going completely dry. "We had a look around at Sunset Rock and along the trail where his body was discovered. Didn't find anything. Olivia is going through the house and shed again to see if she can determine if anything besides his camera is missing."

A sigh echoed across the line. "We may not

find any answers, but I'm afraid this is the best we can do."

The sad truth was the sheriff was right. Sometimes the answers just couldn't be found.

When the call ended, he put one through to Liv. He was too much of a coward to go back and face her again. Mostly because he was damned afraid of what he might say. She didn't answer, so he left a voice mail.

In the end, she was right. There was plenty he could do that didn't involve being in that cabin with her. Willy had friends. Huck intended to interview each one. To stop in all the places he frequented. Talk to anyone who had seen him in the past two or three weeks. What was on his mind? Did he mention any issues? Any trouble with anyone? If Willy had been murdered, murder rarely happened in a vacuum. Someone somewhere had seen or heard something.

All Huck had to do was find that needle in a haystack.

Firefly Lane

As much as she didn't want to, Olivia felt bad for sending Huck away. But she had known that spending so much time with him would have driven her over an edge she might not be able to come back from. It was better if she did this alone. She needed time and space to grieve.

She had decided to start in Willy's bedroom. The room wasn't that large, but it was filled with Gran's treasures. She'd collected flowers, pressed and framed them. They covered a good portion of the walls. Olivia had always loved them. One of the quilts her gran had made covered the bed. Olivia dragged her fingers over the soft, worn cotton. Her grandmother had been a very talented woman. She wondered if her mother had been the same. Olivia remembered glimpses of her mother. She actually had very few memories at all. Gran had talked about her sometimes. Willy said she didn't like talking about Laura because it hurt too much. Olivia hadn't really understood until Huck left. Losing a child was far worse than losing a boyfriend, but afterward Olivia had understood the kind of hurt her gran had suffered.

She picked up the framed photograph of her mother that had sat on the dresser in her grandparents' bedroom for as long as she could remember. Olivia looked so much like her mother. Willy had said she was like Laura's twin. Olivia traced the shape of her mother's face, the silver chain with its tiny sunflower pendant. Willy had given that necklace to Laura on her sixteenth birthday. She'd worn it ever since.

Olivia didn't remember the necklace other than in the pictures of her mother. Laura hadn't really raised her at all. After Olivia was born, Laura had spent more time traveling with Kasey—Olivia's father, though the two had never married—than at home with her new baby daughter. She would put in an appearance, Willy had told Olivia because she certainly didn't remember, only to leave again.

When Olivia was three, her father had left and never come back. Willy said he'd sneaked away, leaving a devastated Laura behind. She was never the same after he left. Then a year later, she died. Photos were Olivia's only real memories of her parents, and she couldn't be sure if she actually recalled those moments or if they were lodged in her subconscious because her grandmother had described the events of each photo to her. As she grew older, Olivia had decided that since Kasey left her, he wasn't worth remembering anyway.

Willy was the only man Olivia had ever loved who hadn't left her.

She closed her eyes and battled a rush of emotion. He would be here now if not for whatever happened up on that ridge. Damn it!

Olivia placed the photograph back where her gran had kept it. The woman in the photo was a stranger, just like the man who'd played the part of her father for just a little while.

One by one, she picked through the drawers in the dresser and bureau as well as the bedside tables. She checked under the bed, under the mattress and in the closet. She straightened up the mess the intruder had made as she went along. Olivia found many things that made her smile, others that made her cry and so many things with which she would never be able to part.

She made up her mind right then that she would leave this cabin exactly as it was. Whenever she was home, she wanted to stay here and be surrounded with all these things.

With a deep, reaffirming breath, she moved on to the bathroom, which was a piece of cake compared to the bedroom. Next, she stared at her own bedroom door. Decided it could wait. She'd spent enough time thinking about Huck the past few hours. Looking at and touching all the things she'd kept from their shared childhood was more than she could deal with just now. Her mother's room was up then.

Olivia opened the door and turned on the light. She moved through the room, checking drawers and shelves. Beneath pillows on the bed and under the mattress. She set to rights the items that had been tossed aside.

When she opened the closet door, her mother's scent, whether real or imagined, filled her nostrils. Her dresses and blouses hung just as they had for more than a quarter century. Shoes lined the closet floor. Olivia slipped her foot into one. She smiled. Fit as if they had belonged to her. A photo of her mother and father together sat on the bureau. It was one of only two or three photos of her dad. She studied the face of the man who had decided she wasn't worth the effort of being a father. Handsome enough. Tall, slim.

Olivia found nothing she hadn't seen before. Noticed nothing missing. She left the room, closing the door firmly behind her.

"Now, for this." She surveyed the main room.

For a moment, the task felt overwhelming, and the idea of where to begin was lost on her. She decided to start with the fireplace and that big old painting of her as a young girl.

Logs were stacked in the fireplace. Even at this time of year there was an occasional cool evening that prompted the need for a cozy fire. She removed the stack, checked beneath the grate. Then moved onto the damper. Nothing except soot.

Using a chair, she reached above the gun rack and hung the painting back in its rightful place. She touched her gran's name where she'd painted it across the bottom right corner. A smile tugged at her lips. Olivia hadn't inherited her grandmother's talent for drawing and painting. She had a pretty good eye when it came to taking pictures but nothing like Willy's.

She climbed down then restacked the logs.

The rest of the main room was still a mess from whoever had ransacked the place. Like in the bedrooms and bath, she straightened up as she went along. She would be staying here until this investigation was over. When she left, she couldn't leave Willy's home in this condition.

Willy hadn't been a focused housekeeper. The dust was a little deep. Olivia grabbed a dust cloth and cleaner and decided she'd better take care of that issue as she went along. Gran would have been appalled. Willy would have said he had other, more urgent matters that needed his attention. Like wandering the trails he so loved.

Olivia understood. Being out there was a calling she couldn't deny either. She loved her work the same way Willy had loved his.

Taking her time, Olivia searched, cleaned

and tidied. By the time she was finished, it was nearly six. Then she whizzed back through the bedrooms and did a little dusting too. Made herself go through her own room. It wasn't until she'd put her cleaning supplies away and washed her hands and face that she realized she hadn't eaten since breakfast. She went back to the fridge and picked through the cheese offerings. Willy had loved cheese, which was good since Olivia loved it too. Crackers were a given. No cheese lover ever allowed himself to run out of crackers.

She hadn't realized she was starving until she dug into the cheese and crackers. While she ate, she thought of the past few conversations with Willy. If there was a problem or if he'd been having trouble with someone, why hadn't he told her? Beyond a bit of noticeable distraction, he'd sounded exactly like he always did. Maybe he hadn't recognized whatever danger was close. He hadn't been a young man anymore.

The thought speared her with pain. She should have come home more often, then she would have seen what he'd obviously hidden from her. Something had been very wrong.

The idea that Father's Day was this month and she'd intended to visit him for that weekend nagged at her. She shouldn't have waited.

Something from Sunday morning's conversation nagged at her. She'd mentioned coming for Father's Day, and he'd suggested she shouldn't. He'd made some excuse about air travel not being as safe as it once was and that they should wait until her birthday in September.

She replayed the conversation. Looking back, it felt off, totally un-Willy-like, that he had urged her so adamantly not to go to the trouble of visiting this month. Why wouldn't he want her to visit?

Tossing her paper plate and napkin into the trash bin, she told herself there must have been a problem. He loved her visits. Hurt twisted inside her at the idea. Maybe it was nothing related to her, but something...related to the person who killed him.

Olivia had to stop herself. Couldn't bear the idea. She would revisit the possibility later. Right now, she needed to finish going through Willy's things. She readied herself to start with the outbuildings. The sooner she was finished, the sooner she could consider whatever she found or felt after having verified what was here and what was not.

Outside, the sun had settled on the treetops, leaving shadows here and there. Olivia started with the barn since that would be easiest. This was where Willy had kept his lawn mower and gardening tools—none of which appeared to have been disturbed. Gran had turned what likely was once a tack room into her personal gardening shed. Her gloves still waited on the wood table where she'd last left them. Her tools and seed pots were perfectly organized. Even the wide-brimmed hat she'd worn faithfully when working outside hung on its hook. She'd repeated the rules of proper outdoor work attire to Olivia a thousand times. Sunscreen, a hat, gloves, good jeans and sturdy shoes.

Olivia touched the gloves but didn't pick them up. Willy wouldn't have wanted her to move them from that exact spot. The dust gathered around them was proof he'd been very careful not to disturb those gloves either.

Nothing in the barn that hadn't always been there. Nothing missing.

The shed was next.

Olivia had been inside it already when she'd had a quick look to see if anything was missing, so the multitude of familiar scents didn't hit her quite so hard this time. She focused on Gran's studio first. It was on the south side of the shed, with windows on three sides facing south, west and east. Until darkness fell, some amount of light filtered into the large room. Willy had given his wife the larger portion of the shed. The brushes and materials she had used lined the shelves along the walls beneath the windows. A large work table held court in the middle of the room. Gran's easel stood near a wall of windows. Waiting on the easel was a nearly finished painting of a scene in Coolidge Park—one of Chattanooga's most beloved places.

A customer had commissioned the painting and would gladly have taken it without the final touches remaining, but Willy had refused to part with his wife's final work. Olivia was glad he hadn't. It looked perfect standing on the easel in Gran's studio. She was very grateful the painting had not been overturned or damaged during the intruder's rampage of a search.

Olivia prowled through the drawers in the wood table. She opened wooden boxes Gran used for storage and checked behind every single item cluttering the endless shelves in the studio. She tidied any mess made by the intruder as she went along. Nothing unexpected was found. Nothing missing as far as she could determine. On to Willy's side of the structure.

Willy's workroom and darkroom were closed off from the rest of the shed. The only entrance into the shed led into a small sort of foyer where there was a bench and a place to hang a coat or umbrella. A fridge stocked with water and soft drinks sat in one corner. There was a small bathroom.

Straight ahead was the set of French doors that led to Gran's studio. On the north side was the single door to Willy's work area. The space beyond was plain, no frills. A typical photographer's studio sans the backdrops since he never did personal portraits. A high table extended the length of one wall. Willy's computers and printers sat humming, ready to wake up with a single touch. Two stools, one at each work station, waited. Filing cabinets and shelves lined another wall.

This tidying and in-depth search were going to take some time.

Olivia started with the computers. She scanned the folders on both. Found nothing but the usual landscape photos. Willy didn't do people. If a person was in the shot he wanted, he waited until they moved on before taking it.

Nothing unexpected in his email.

She checked the shelves, reorganizing as she went. Moved the few items that hadn't been disturbed and carefully placed them back where they belonged. Then the file cabinets. She opened drawer after drawer, reviewing the contents of each folder it contained. Nothing she hadn't expected to find. She was very grateful the intruder had not slung files all over the room. He'd apparently run out of steam by the time he reached the shed. His search had cooled noticeably.

The darkroom was next. It was small, so maybe it wouldn't take so long.

She reached for the narrow door. It was locked.

She shook her head. Of course it was. Willy always kept that room locked. She took a moment to remember where he kept the key hidden.

A grin stretched across her face. "Oh yeah."

She walked back to the more vintage of the two computers, picked up the keyboard and there was the key. Taped to the bottom of the keyboard. Willy kept one in his pocket, but he also kept this spare just in case he lost the one he carried around all the time.

She walked in, turned on the light. There was nothing out of place in here since the door had been locked. The darkroom was divided into two parts, the dry side and the wet side. The dry side, enlarger and cutter along with the paper storage area were straightforward, easy to scan. The wet side was a little more complicated with its various trays. Developer, stop bath, fixer and water and then the drying area.

Olivia found nothing beyond the expected.

Until she reached the end of the drying area, where Willy had hung what were likely his most recent photos. Or at least the ones he'd taken and then developed before his death.

The photos were all hanging backward with the plain white paper side facing out instead of the image captured by the film.

Why would he do that? He always hung them so he could view the images.

Olivia reached out and turned around the first of the row of six photos. The image appeared to be in downtown Chattanooga. It was taken at night, but she could see a bar in the background. Not the kind she would imagine Willy ever visiting. But the most surprising part was the person—a man—near the entrance of the bar. She couldn't make out his face. Tall. Thin. He wore a T-shirt and jeans and a baseball cap.

She turned the next photo. Same general area. Same man based on the tee and cap. The photo was of him coming out of the bar. His face was still too blurry to make out. All six of the photos were of this man. The final one showed him climbing into a black car parked along the street. Unfortunately, the license plate was not visible.

Heart thumping extra hard, Olivia removed the photos, placed them in a stack. These definitely warranted additional consideration. Before leaving the darkroom, she checked the shelves under the tables. Moved the jugs of chemicals around to see anything else that might be stashed there. Nothing.

On her way out of the darkroom, she grabbed the loupe.

The thought occurred to her that she should call Huck, but she couldn't go there just yet. She needed a little more distance.

Outside, it was dark now. She hurried across the backyard and entered through the mudroom door. Closing the door with her foot, she still managed to lose her hold on the photographs, and they flew across the floor.

"Oh damn." She set the loupe aside, flipped on the mudroom light and dropped to her knees to gather the potential evidence. As she did, she scolded herself for forgetting to lock up the darkroom. She'd have to go back.

A solid thud echoed from somewhere deeper in the house.

Olivia froze.

Had she locked the front door before going out to the shed? No, of course not. Other than the darkroom, Willy rarely locked his doors as long as he was home. She'd grown up with the idea that it was safe to leave your doors unlocked, and although she didn't do that in

Bozeman or any of the other places she had lived, being back here had her falling into old habits.

Big mistake.

Someone was in the house.

Her heart launched into her throat. Her fingers loosened on the photographs she'd started to pick up. Slowly, she pushed to her feet. Listening intently for any other sound. Maybe when she'd closed the door she caused something to fall...

But she hadn't closed the door that hard... had she?

The silence throbbed in time with her rising respiration.

A slam made her jerk.

Door.

Front door.

Someone had either gone out...or come in.

Olivia grabbed the knob on the back door and twisted, opened the door and rushed out into the darkness.

She hid next to the steps, crouched and pressed against the stone foundation. *Listen! Listen*, she told herself, forcing her heart to slow and the roar of blood to quiet.

For a very long while, she remained in that crouched position. Listening. Not one thing disrupted the usual night sounds. Crickets.

Frogs. The hoot of an owl. The whisper of a rare breeze.

When enough time had passed that she felt it was safe to move, Olivia dared to rise. Her legs were stiff from squatting for so long.

Slowly, she moved around the house, peering into the darkness. No other vehicles except her car and the Defender. No sounds beyond the ones she had long minutes ago identified.

Holding her breath, she climbed the steps to the front porch. A creak from the last one made her freeze.

When nothing or no one moved or made a sound, she crossed the porch. The door was closed. She reached for the knob but froze.

Someone had been in the house. Not the wind. Not some animal.

A person. One capable of opening the door and then slamming it shut.

She opened the door and stepped inside. The house was dark save for the dim mudroom light reaching through the kitchen. She felt her way to the corner behind the door. When her fingers closed around the cool steel of the shotgun, relief washed through her.

Shotgun in hand, she moved to the switch and flipped on the light.

Olivia blinked rapidly to adjust her eyes to

the brightness. She surveyed the main room. Everything looked exactly as she'd left it.

Her first deep breath since hearing that thud filled her lungs.

"Okay." She closed and locked the front door. Walked straight to the mudroom and closed and locked that one. She gathered the photographs and loupe and moved back to the main room. She placed the potential evidence or whatever it was on the table and did what she had to do.

She lifted the shotgun into firing position, then progressed through the rest of the house to ensure there was no one hiding inside. She didn't expect there was, but she had to be sure. A quick look into closets and under beds…behind the shower curtain confirmed her conclusion.

Then she got angry.

What the hell was going on here?

She stamped back to the table where she'd left those photographs.

Olivia placed the shotgun on the table in easy reach, then she sat down and spread out the six eight-by-tens. She picked up the one that showed the man's face and grabbed the loupe. Still, his face was too blurred to make out. Willy must have taken the photos from quite a distance.

She moved from photo to photo, scanning each closely with the loupe.

Going back to the photo that showed the man's face the clearest, which wasn't clear at all, she studied the rest of him. The tee he wore sported a football team logo. His button-down shirt with its multicolored checks was open, worn more like a jacket. She traced over his face again.

She stared at the bar front in the photo and what she could see of the street. Why would Willy have been following some guy around in a not-so-good part of downtown?

Didn't make a lot of sense.

But neither did his falling from a place he loved and had visited thousands of times.

She turned to the front door.

Had the man in these photos been in the house tonight?

Were these photos what he was looking for? If so, why not go to the shed and break into the darkroom?

Or maybe he didn't know about the photos and had come back to look for whatever he'd been searching for when he tore the house apart.

He would have seen her car and how the house had been straightened up, but that hadn't deterred him.

Ice slid through her veins.

She reached for her phone and called Huck.

As much as she didn't want to, she needed him.

Chapter Five

Huck barreled down the drive and slid to a stop. He was already opening the door when he shoved the car into Park and shut off the engine.

Olivia stood in the open doorway, that old shotgun hanging from her hands. He ran toward her, fear—no, terror—about what could have happened pounding through his veins. He shouldn't have left her here alone.

He wasn't letting her out of his sight again. Not until this was done.

"Whoever was here," she said as he strode toward her, "he's gone now."

Relief that she was okay almost buckled his knees. "I need to double check."

She nodded. "I'll just…" She backed up, moving deeper into the room and then to the wall next to the door. She leaned against it. "I'll wait here."

He closed and locked the front door. "I'd feel better if you stuck with me."

Another feeble nod.

Damn. She was scared to death. He could understand why. This cabin was basically in the middle of nowhere. No neighbors for miles.

She couldn't stay here. He would not allow her to stay here. Not alone. Whether she liked it or not—whether she agreed with him or not, she was not spending another moment alone.

He moved through the house. Checked each room. She'd put things back in order. Terror still stabbed at him whenever he thought of her being here alone and someone coming in the house. Willy would have been as mad as hell at him for leaving her here alone. He should never have allowed that to happen. But she'd insisted. Wanted him to go. Damn it.

The house was clear. Relief rushed through him. She was okay, and that was what mattered. He wouldn't make that mistake again.

He hesitated in the kitchen. "Stay put. I'll check the shed and barn. Keep the doors locked and don't open them for any reason—not unless I tell you to."

She stared at him a moment as if she might argue with the order, then she said, "Okay."

His reached for the door when what he really wanted to do was hug her and promise her everything would be okay, but he couldn't make that promise just yet. He flipped a pair of switches at the back door and headed out. He waited on the steps until he heard the lock turn.

Willy had installed a few outdoor lights decades ago, but the illumination was minimal. His wife had insisted she didn't want anything interfering with her ability to see the stars.

"Stars are about the only thing you can see," Huck muttered as he navigated the darkness. He pulled the handgun from his waistband and held it, barrel down, as he moved forward.

It wasn't like crossing the backyard was a straight shot. The flower and vegetable gardens Olivia's grandparents had cultivated over the years spanned the distance between the house and the tree lines on the property. Little fences and stone borders created a damned maze. Huck had known this place like the back of his hand before.

But that had been a long time ago. Now he had to pay attention to each step to prevent himself from tripping and falling into a mass of thorny rose bushes or a vine-covered obelisk. The gate to the small fenced area around the barn stood open. At one time, there were chickens and goats. When Huck had moved back last fall, he'd asked Willy about the critters—as he had called them—and Willy had chuckled and said he'd managed to outlive them all.

Anger sparked deep inside Huck at the idea that someone had ended the man's life. The world needed more folks like Willy.

The barn was clear. Huck stayed alert to the slightest sound or movement as he headed for the shed. Inside, he turned on the lights. Maybe two minutes were required to determine there was no one hiding out there either.

It appeared Olivia was right. Whoever had been here was gone now.

He weaved his way through the gardens and to the back door and gave it a knock. "It's me. You can open up now."

The lock released and the door opened immediately. "Did you see anyone?"

He shook his head as he stepped inside. "Whoever it was is either long gone or hiding out there in the darkness somewhere." He tucked his weapon away, closed the door and locked it. "I didn't notice any vehicles on the side of the road as I drove here and I didn't meet any outgoing vehicles, but that doesn't mean someone didn't park on one of the side roads along the main route and walk over."

"There's something you need to see." She propped the shotgun against the wall and walked to the table. "I found these hanging in the darkroom. They must be the last photos Willy developed."

Huck picked up one and then the next. He recognized the area. "Downtown. Not the sort of places I'd expect Willy to venture into."

"He was watching that man, I think." She picked up the loupe. "His face is not clear enough for me to make out. Maybe you'll recognize him."

Huck used the loupe to study the images of the man, particularly his face. Olivia was right; it was impossible to ID him. He placed the final photo and the loupe on the table. "Why would Willy be following some guy—anyone, for that matter?"

Olivia shook her head and settled into a chair. "I have no idea. He never took photos of people." She shrugged. "I mean, besides family and that wasn't as often as one would think given he carried that camera with him all the time and everywhere. It was like part of him."

Huck lowered into the seat at the end of the table. "I don't think I ever saw him without it."

Olivia rubbed at her eyes and exhaled a weary breath. "I don't understand what's happening."

"We'll figure this out," he promised, knowing he might not be able to keep that promise. "Tomorrow, we'll drive to the bar in the photos and have a look around. Maybe talk to the owner or manager."

"I don't want to wait." She stood. "I'm going now."

Oh, hell. He'd figured that was what she'd say. He pushed to his feet. "I know better than to try and talk you out of it."

"Thanks."

"So I'm going with you."

"I don't need a bodyguard," she countered, anger or frustration in her voice.

"Maybe not," he said, pushing in his chair, "but this is my case, and that means I'm in charge."

The stare-off lasted a full fifteen seconds.

"Fine." She walked over to where she'd left the shotgun, picked it up and returned it to its resting place above the mantel. "Just make sure you don't get in my way."

There was the Liv he knew and...

The thought trailed off. "We'll play it by ear, how about that?"

She didn't answer, just grabbed her bag and started for the front door.

Outside, she locked up and headed for his SUV. She opened her own door and climbed in. Huck shrugged, walked around the hood and got in on his side. She'd never liked him playing the part of gentleman. *I can open my own door*, she'd scolded. *I can close it too. I'm not helpless, Huck.*

Olivia hadn't been the kind of girl who wanted anyone doing for her what she could do herself. Apparently, that hadn't changed.

But she definitely wasn't a girl anymore.

He glanced at her as he drove through the night, heading down the mountain.

Willy swore she hadn't had a single serious relationship since Huck left. But maybe the old guy had only told Huck what he wanted to hear. As far as he could see, her personal life had remained personal. Her social media was all about work. He'd been cyberstalking her for years. At first, he hadn't been able to bear seeing her even online. Eventually, his curiosity or need—maybe both—had gotten the better of him, and he'd found her. His own social media account was just a page he'd opened in order to see her. He never posted anything. Had no desire to interact with anyone else. She had been the one and only reason he'd bothered.

"Willy said you don't do relationships."

Her words startled him. He'd been in his own thoughts so long, his focus on driving, he'd almost forgotten he wasn't alone. "What?"

Had she asked Willy about him?

"You know Willy," she said, her attention remaining straight ahead. "He never stopped seeing you as part of the family. Sometimes he'd just start talking about you."

Huck got it now. "Even when you didn't want to hear it."

Her silence was answer enough.

"He talked about you all the time." Huck smiled. He couldn't tell her how much he'd loved hearing about her adventures. Even before he moved back, the phone conversations he and Willy had always somehow found their way to the subject of Olivia.

"I miss him."

Her voice sounded so desolate, so weary. It took every ounce of willpower he possessed not to reach for her hand. But she wouldn't appreciate the comfort. Not from him.

"You didn't answer the question."

He glanced at her profile. "You didn't ask a question."

"Is it true, you don't do relationships?"

He'd known that was what she meant, but he wasn't sure confirming or denying Willy's statement would be a good thing. As strong as Huck wanted to believe he was, he did have feelings, and if there was anyone on this earth capable of making him weak or causing him pain, it was her.

"Define *relationship*," he said instead.

She gave a dry laugh. "Seriously, you can't just say yes or no?"

She was looking at him now. He felt her gaze burning through him. When he braked for a red light, he dared to meet her fierce glare. "Does it matter?"

She blinked, turned her head to stare forward once more. "Not at all."

And there it was, a blade to the heart. "Enough said."

The rest of the drive was made in silence.

Even on a Tuesday night, traffic was frustrating. Chattanooga was a beautiful city with numerous tourist activities and plenty of old South charm, but it also had its share of problems, including traffic and road work. And like any other large metropolitan area, there were areas that were far less safe than others. Their destination, Rick's Bar and Grill, was in one of those areas.

He parked on the street, half a block from the bar. Based on the view from there, Willy had been parked in the same general area.

"I want to go inside."

He'd seen that one coming. "Chances of catching our unidentified subject in there aren't that good."

She turned to him. It was too dark to make out her expression, but he felt her glare. "I snapped pics of the guy in Willy's photos. Maybe someone in there, a bartender or waitress, will recognize our unsub." She stared at the bar. "I've watched my share of cop shows too."

Now she'd gone and ticked him off. "First of all," he pointed out, "this is not the kind of place where folks willingly ID each other." She started to argue, but he held up a hand cutting her off. "Secondly, I *am* a cop."

Rather than toss a biting comeback, she surprised him by simply getting out of the vehicle.

"Damn it." He grabbed the badge from his console and got out. "Hold up, Liv." He tugged his shirttail from his jeans to cover the weapon tucked at the small of his back. Slipped his badge into his front pocket.

She didn't wait.

He hustled to catch up with her. "You need to cool down."

"I'm fine."

He snagged her by the arm, pulled her to a stop. She shot him a how-dare-you look. "This is not some mountainside where ancient civilizations once resided, or some valley where parts of a lost city are thought to be, this is a place where people hook up for drugs and other commodities, make the kind of deals no one wants to know about. The kind of place where people end up dead."

She jerked her arm loose from his grip. "I'm not naive, Huck. I know what happens on the streets in crime-infested areas." She glanced at his untucked shirt. "I also know that weapon, as well as the badge you're carrying, makes you a far bigger target than me."

With that she stalked away. He followed. Anything else he might have said was irrelevant considering she wouldn't listen.

The vibration of the music shook the air well before they reached the entrance. Inside, the joint was packed with bodies and the music was even louder than he'd expected. The tables were full, the stools at the bar as well. The rest of the crowd filled the space between the bar and tables. No doubt several city ordinances were being broken, including local fire codes.

A big sign over the bar announced the grill part of the establishment was no longer operating. No surprise there. Food wasn't the moneymaker in a place like this.

Olivia slipped through the crowd as if she did this every day. She reached the bar, and he moved in behind her. She stiffened at his nearness, but she didn't look back or say anything. Not that he would have heard her or that it would have done her any good.

She waved down the first of two bartenders. Showed him the photos. He shook his head.

Huck stood by while she repeated the process with the other bartender. Then they moved to the end of the bar where the waitresses picked up their orders. Olivia did the same with each one. Got a similar head shake in response.

Huck watched the waitresses. Only one captured his interest. Blond. Skinny. Pamela, according to her name tag.

Pamela had recognized something about the pics. Huck had spotted the tells when she looked at the pics and then shook her head. She'd lied straight up.

Luckily, a couple of stools at the bar became available. Huck slid atop one first, his gaze clocking Pamela's movements.

The bartender arrived, and he ordered beers.

Olivia shot him a look and leaned close enough for him to hear, "I still don't like beer."

He turned to her, putting his face so close to hers their noses almost touched. Heat seared through him, but he managed to deliver the necessary question. "Does this look like a wine kind of place to you?"

She leaned away and faced forward.

The bartender plopped two bottles of beer on the counter. Huck picked up one and pushed a bill toward him, then turned back to his study of the waitress. She noticed him watching and smiled. He smiled back.

Half a beer later, she had left her tray at the end of the counter and headed down a corridor marked Restrooms and Emergency Exit.

Huck leaned toward Olivia. "I'll be right back."

She jumped as if his voice had startled her. She turned toward him. "Where are you going?"

He nodded to the corridor where Pamela had disappeared. "Bathroom. Do not move from this barstool. Stay put right here where the bartenders can see you."

She rolled her eyes. "Where would I go?"

"Seriously, Liv," he pressed her with his eyes, "don't move."

She picked up her beer and took a sip. Made a face. "Go."

He slid off the stool and shouldered through the crowd of patrons. The corridor was empty. The emergency exit was propped open with a rock. Huck figured that was where she'd headed. Maybe for a smoke break.

As much as he didn't like leaving Liv at the bar, he suspected the waitress wasn't going to talk if they both appeared to gang up on her.

He glanced beyond the crack that separated the door from its frame. Sure enough, the waitress was leaning against the wall, sucking on a cigarette. He put his shoulder into the door, opening it and surveying right and left as he did. The back side of the establishment was fairly well lit, and he spotted no other warm bodies in the vicinity.

He walked to where Pamela stood and propped his back against the wall, matching her stance.

"Your friend didn't come with you?" She turned to Huck, blew smoke in his face.

He waved it away. "You know the guy we're looking for." Not a question. She recognized him.

She turned her head, staring at the back of the row of businesses that faced the next street. "I saw him a couple of times."

"You know his name?"

"Nope." Another long drag. "Only saw him here twice."

"Did you talk to him?"

"Maybe."

"Was he with anyone?" Huck resisted the urge to warn her that he could haul her in for questioning if she didn't cooperate.

"Nope."

"What will it cost me to find out what you talked about?"

She grinned. "Your friend wouldn't be happy if you gave me what I wanted." She glanced at his lower anatomy.

Huck chuckled. "Is there a compromise?"

She threw down her cigarette. Smashed it out

with the toe of her high-heeled shoe. Then she turned to him. "He was looking for a woman."

The answer could mean a number of things. "A particular woman?"

She nodded. "From his description and the photo he flashed me, I'd say he was looking for your friend."

Pamela stepped around him and went back inside.

Huck surveyed the alley again and then did the same. His mind screamed at him that she couldn't be right. Why would some random guy come here looking for Olivia? She hadn't lived in the Chattanooga area in more than a decade. And she had never been to a place like this one.

He cut through the crowd and found his way to the bar.

But Olivia wasn't there.

His heart punched his sternum. He twisted around, scanned the crowd. Swore. Where the hell was she?

He plowed through the crowd, searching for her white blouse. The one that he'd tried not to notice stretching over her breasts and molding tightly around her waist. The one he'd wanted to tear off her.

Fear rose like a snake ready to strike as he searched face after face. No Olivia. Damn it!

Long dark hair. White blouse.

He spotted her talking to a guy not ten feet from the front entrance. His fear turned to fury.

He strode straight up to her and took her by the arm. "We have to go."

She glared up at him. "What are you doing?"

The other man stepped forward. Huck cut him a look and warned, "Don't even think about it."

The other guy held up a hand then dissolved into the crowd.

Smart man.

"Let's go."

She ranted at him as he ushered her toward the door, but he couldn't hear the words over the music.

As soon as they were outside and the doors closed, muffling the volume of the music, she dug in her heels. "What the hell, Huck?"

"We'll talk in a minute." He started forward again.

She didn't budge, forcing him to stop.

"What did the waitress say?"

Maybe she had watched a lot of cop shows. "Not here," he urged.

This time she complied and started walking again.

He watched the street, the sidewalk and

storefronts as they moved quickly to his SUV.
He touched the passenger-side door handle and
the lock disengaged. Thankfully she didn't
make a fuss, so he opened the door for her to
climb in. Then he closed her door and hurried
around to the driver's side. He slid behind the
wheel but didn't start talking until they were
back on the road and heading up the mountain. He focused on driving and ensuring that
no one had followed them.

When her patience reached its limit, she
turned to him. "What did she say?"

"How do you know I spoke to anyone?" He
really wanted to know the answer. He was cu-
rious.

"The mirror behind the bar. I saw you watching her. Saw her watching back. Obviously, the
fact that she had to go to the bathroom at the
same time as you was no coincidence."

He grinned. "Pamela and I met out back."

"That's not sketchy at all," she muttered.

Was that jealousy he heard in her voice? He
wished. "I recognized she was lying when you
asked her if she knew the guy in the photos."

"And?"

"She didn't know his name, but she'd seen
him at the bar a couple of times. She said he
was looking for someone."

Olivia shifted in the seat. "Who? Not Willy. I can't see him at a dive bar."

Huck wasn't sure how to tell her the rest. "A woman. He was looking for a woman."

"Did *Pamela* know the woman's name?" Olivia demanded. "Good grief, are you purposely trying to be evasive?"

Huck braced himself. "He didn't give a name, just a description."

"How is that helpful?" She sank back into the seat. "I do not understand what's happening. None of this makes sense."

The solitary answer he hadn't given her yet wasn't going to help her understand any more than the revelation had him.

"So tell me," she insisted, "what did this woman he was asking about look like?"

Huck braked at the four-way stop. He turned to her and prepared to say the words that, he feared, wouldn't help at all yet would somehow change everything.

"You. The waitress said the woman he asked about looked like you."

Chapter Six

Olivia didn't speak again until he parked in front of her grandfather's cabin.

She had never been in that bar. She did not know the man in the blurry photos or the waitress named Pamela. Why on earth would the man—this stranger Willy had been watching—have gone to that bar looking for *her*?

It made absolutely no sense. Willy would never be involved with whatever this stranger was up to. Willy would have gone to the police if there was trouble he could pinpoint and prove.

Her mind stumbled on the thought. Then why watch the guy?

What she and Huck had learned tonight hadn't provided any answers...only more questions.

"We should get your bag," Huck said, his voice too soft, too quiet. "You can't stay here."

Olivia glared at him even though he wouldn't see her in the dark. She wanted to yell at him, but she was too emotionally drained. "No. If he—whoever he is—comes back, he'll come here. This is where I need to be."

Huck stared out the windshield for a moment, then turned to her, his expression unreadable in the darkness. "If you're staying, I'm staying."

What could she say to that? She was the one who had called him for help. Even if she so, so wanted to do this without his or anyone else's help, she understood she could not do this alone. Only a fool would pretend otherwise.

"Fine. You can sleep on the couch."

She pushed the door open and got out. She might have to be under the same roof as him, but she didn't have to look at him or endure the scent of him. It was driving her mad.

She did not want to feel that hunger…that need for him.

It had taken her years, but she had finally broken herself of that need. Like an addict who'd survived the pain of withdrawal, she'd put that craving behind her. He was no longer her first thought when she woke in the morning. No longer her last thought before she went to sleep at night. No longer a part of every breath she took.

She refused to become that person again—the one who could hardly bear to live without him.

No. No. No!

She unlocked the door and left it open since he was right behind her. Didn't look back. She went straight to her bedroom and slammed the door shut. Collapsing against the door, she squeezed her eyes shut to block the renewed flood of emotions.

She would not cry anymore. No amount of tears would bring Willy back or solve the mystery of his death. Being strong was the only way to move forward, and damn it, she intended to move forward. To find answers. Strength was the only weapon she had against whatever was happening here.

Willy always told her she was one of the strongest people he knew. She could not let him down now.

Olivia opened her eyes and felt for the switch. She flipped it, and light filled the room. Her childhood room...the one where she'd always felt safe and loved. The one she'd tidied and dusted only a few hours ago.

She blinked, looked again at the wall over her bed where a poster of her favorite rock band had resided since she was seventeen. The poster had been torn away and now lay draped over her headboard with only one corner left clinging to a strip of tape on the wall. Words had been painted on the bared wall:

I knew you'd come back.

Feeling as if she were in a bad dream, Olivia moved toward the bed, her gaze holding to the words. She reached out, touched the black letters that had obviously been spray-painted above her headboard.

Dry. They had been there for a while. An hour at least. Whoever had done this had come into the house while they were gone. Unlocked the door and then locked it back. Surely, he wouldn't have dared to do all this with Olivia right outside in the shed cleaning up his mess…her heart pounded harder. Either way… he had been back.

"Huck!"

His name erupted from her in a final wail before every ounce of remaining strength and will poured out of her. She wilted against her bed.

What was happening?

The door flew open, banged against the wall, and he was suddenly at her side, staring at the ominous message. "What the hell?"

"We locked both the front and back doors."

Olivia turned to the man standing next to her. "He must have Willy's key."

"You shouldn't stay here tonight, Liv."

A blast of fury shored up her failing strength. "I'm staying."

He exhaled a weary breath. Reached for his cell. "I have to call this in. Get someone from the CSI team out here."

Olivia left the room and moved through the rest of the house. Had anything been taken? Had he returned to the house for something he'd hoped to find that he hadn't found last time? Or only to leave her a message?

When she felt satisfied that nothing had been moved, she went to the kitchen and readied a pot of coffee. Obviously, sleep would have to wait.

Huck joined her as she leaned against the counter, waiting for the coffee to brew.

"It'll be about an hour before someone can get here."

"I can't imagine what they'll find," she said, frustrated beyond all reason. "Obviously this guy is smart enough to cover up his tracks."

"Maybe so but we have to look all the same. I need to have a look around outside. I'd prefer it if you stuck with me."

"Let's do it." She'd already looked around inside. He'd done the same after making his call. Beyond the two of them, there was no one in the house.

Huck headed outside, she followed.

"Stay close," he warned.

"I know the drill." By now she was becoming an expert at this sort of thing.

The shed was first. If anyone had been inside, they hadn't moved anything. Hadn't touched anything. Olivia followed him to the barn, her mind mulling over the details of the photos. If the man's face were clearer, maybe Huck could have run the image through some sort of system that would ID him. He likely had a driver's license, possibly a criminal record. Then again, that might only happen in fiction.

The idea was irrelevant when considered against the question that had just occurred to her.

Willy was a true professional—an artist. How had he taken such a bad shot six times? Olivia had never known him to fail to home in on any scene he chose. The photos of the man at the bar were wrong. So, so wrong.

When Huck was satisfied no one was lurking in the shed or barn, they returned to the house. The guy from the crime-scene team arrived earlier than expected. The smell of coffee summoned her as they went back inside. Huck and the other guy, Sergeant David Snelling, got straight down to business. Snelling was a large man, six three or four, broad shoulders. Dark hair peppered with gray. Most importantly, he appeared very thorough.

Exhausted, Olivia poured herself a cup of the coffee and waited. She sipped the brew and mulled over the myriad questions whirling in her brain. Why hadn't Willy told her there was something going on? Then she reminded herself that he never complained. Never talked about feeling bad or getting old. He'd insisted he was going to live forever. He'd been telling her that since she was nine, when Gran died. He would never leave her. He would live forever.

Except he hadn't.

The burn of tears rimmed her eyes. She squeezed them shut and focused on the rich, hot coffee. She had to use whatever was necessary to keep herself grounded. Someone had pushed Willy. She was certain. She had to find that person. Had to ensure he paid for what he'd done.

It wouldn't bring Willy back, but it was the right thing to do. Willy deserved justice.

Olivia inhaled a deep breath, forced the thoughts away for now. She finished her coffee, left the mug in the sink and went to the bookcase that sat beneath the television. She sat down on the floor and pulled out the family photo albums her gran had made when Olivia was a kid. Willy never did photo albums. No matter that he took thousands of photographs. They were either on the wall or neatly tucked away in chronological order out in the studio.

She opened the oldest one first. Photos of her grandparents and her mother filled page after page. Willy had been an extraordinarily handsome man in his youth. Still had been, in Olivia's opinion. She wondered why he'd never dated or even sought out companionship after so many years. Especially after Olivia moved away. She remembered asking him once if he was lonely. Willy had laughed and said that loneliness was only a state of mind. He filled his life with the beautiful things around him and with capturing that beauty on film.

Had he only been saying what she wanted to hear? That he was fine without her?

She stared at the photos of her mother. She had been so much prettier than Olivia. Everyone who saw the photos always said she and her mother looked alike, but Olivia had never seen herself in that league. Her mother had been stunningly beautiful. There weren't that many photos of her father. Only the two. He'd been quite handsome as well, with a wide, teasing smile.

Olivia hadn't really thought about him since she was a child, but she considered him now. Where did he live? Was he still alive? Why had he left them? Her grandparents hadn't talked about him either. Whenever Olivia had asked, they would only say that he'd been a drifter. Had no family except for Olivia and her mother. Unfortunately, his inability to form roots had caused him to drift on when Olivia was still a toddler.

She wondered if her mother had grieved over being left behind by the man she loved. Had she grieved herself to death the way Gran had after she died? Olivia wasn't convinced of the idea, but she couldn't deny there appeared to be scientific evidence that dying of a broken heart was indeed possible.

Turning the page, she studied the photos of herself growing up. So many included Huck. She smiled. Couldn't help herself. They'd fallen in love as kids even before they had a clue what that kind of love was. She moved to the final album. The photos there took her breath. The two of them were always together. She had thought they always would be.

The front door closed, and Olivia jumped.

"He'll get back to us if there's any news," Huck said.

She hadn't realized he and Snelling, who had obviously just left, had even walked through the room where she was sitting, deep in the past.

Emerging fully back to the present, she tucked the photo albums away. "Good." Then she stood. "I've been thinking—"

Huck said the same thing. They looked at each other and laughed. "You first," he insisted.

"There has to be some sort of personal connection to all this." Her heart squeezed at the thought of sweet Willy lying in the morgue on an ice-cold slab. She blinked away the image. "Whoever hurt Willy had an agenda. Wanted something. Whatever that something was, only Willy could provide it, which is why I believe the killer was someone Willy knew. Maybe even trusted considering they were on that ridge together when he fell."

"Assuming Willy went there willingly on the day of his death," Huck countered.

Olivia gave a nod. "It kills me to look at the possibility in that light, but you're correct."

Huck went to the coffee pot, picked up a mug and filled it. "Bearing in mind tonight's message," he set his attention on her, "my guess is whatever the trouble was—it was about you."

The concept ripped through her. "I've been skipping all around that scenario, not wanting to land on it."

"You haven't lived in the area for a long while now," he said as he propped a hip against the counter, "which suggests it probably doesn't have anything to do with anyone here."

"No one here would hurt Willy," she granted. Not possible. Willy had no enemies.

"I agree," Huck confirmed. "I interviewed several people today, and no one was aware of Willy having any sort of trouble. All said the same thing: Same old Willy. Good man. Nobody was aware of any issues."

She nodded. "It's hard to see anything else at this point."

"Which makes me seriously nervous," Huck said, "about you staying here."

"We've settled that already," she reminded him, not going there again.

"Got it," he assented.

She thought about those last conversations she'd had with Willy and that message left on her bedroom wall. "I told Willy I was coming to visit for Father's Day, but he was adamant that I shouldn't come. He came up with all the reasons it would be better if I didn't. I didn't think too much about it at the time, but now I don't know."

"Whatever was going on," Huck said, "Willy didn't want you involved or didn't want this person to be able to get to you."

Several things clicked in Olivia's brain just then. "Wait." She rushed over to the refrigerator, searched the notes secured to the door with magnets. "It's not here." She turned to face Huck. "Willy had my cell number and address on the fridge, just in case he got sick… or something happened. I insisted that he keep it there. It's gone."

Coffee forgotten, Huck joined her at the fridge and scanned the notes there as well. "Where else would he have had something about where you live now?"

She rushed to the drawer where envelopes and postage stamps were kept. There was an old address book there too. Gran had kept it there for as long as Olivia could remember. She flipped to the page where her name and information would be and it was gone. Torn out.

She showed it to Huck. "He was hiding my contact info."

The idea that Willy was murdered to ensure Olivia came back tore through her like an axe to the chest.

"What do you know about your father?" Huck asked before she could voice the terrifying idea.

Olivia shook her head, mostly because she couldn't bear the scenario circling her brain. "No more than you, really. He and my mother met when she was away at college. She got pregnant with me, dropped out and brought him home with her. When I was three, he disappeared and then she died." Olivia struggled to keep her throat from closing with the emotion swelling inside her. She couldn't be the reason Willy was dead. How would she endure that?

"Willy never heard from him again?" Huck tilted his head, eyeing her as if he suspected she was on the verge of breaking down. "No letters? No pop ins? You were his daughter, after all."

"Nothing that I know about." She swallowed at the tightness growing in her throat.

Huck scrubbed a hand over his jaw. "Was there ever any legal paperwork done about you? Custody papers? Adoption?"

Olivia moistened her lips, struggled to stay calm. "My parents never married, so I didn't have his last name. But his name is on my birth certificate. Kasey Aldean. There was never any other paperwork to my knowledge."

"We need to see if we can find him." Huck shrugged. "Rule him out."

"I guess so." She drew in a deep breath. Somehow managed to calm her heart. "I can't see why he'd come around after all this time."

"You never know. He may have been in jail most of the time he's been gone. He was aware Willy was quite the famous photographer. Maybe he wanted money. Or maybe he just finally grew up and wanted to know his daughter."

"That's a lot of maybes." Though she hadn't really known her father, she doubted he'd suddenly felt the urge to be a father and get to know his daughter.

The thought had her considering how Willy might have reacted had the man showed up. He would not have been happy…he would have taken measures to protect Olivia. Like hiding her contact information.

"The real question," Huck said, "is if the guy did show up, why didn't Willy tell you?"

"What if he was trying to protect me?" That fear pounded in her veins again. "What if he's dead because of me?"

"Don't do that to yourself, Liv."

Olivia didn't see him move, but he felt closer somehow. "But if—"

"You're tired," he interrupted her. "We should call it a night. I'll blockade the doors and be on the couch if you need me."

Whether it was out of a need to distract herself from thoughts she couldn't bear or sheer stupidity, she asked, "Why did you come back? Really?"

He searched her eyes, her face. "Does it matter? Really?"

Rather than answer, she forged on, "Did you have a bad breakup? Couldn't see your way past it to hang around in Miami? Let's face it, that's a big move just to take care of the homeplace. Weren't you up for a promotion or something?"

Those blue eyes of his narrowed suspiciously.

She'd said too much. She hadn't meant to reveal how Willy kept her up-to-date on Huck, even when she hadn't wanted to hear it. Damn it. She should have shut up and gone to bed. She should have let the awful possibilities haunt her rather than end up standing here having said what she said. Damn it.

"Why *didn't* you come back?" he asked.

She held steady, didn't look away as that piercing gaze bored into hers. If she evaded the truth, he would know it. Obviously, he'd honed that skill in his work. "I've thought about it the past couple of years." She looked away then, couldn't endure his probing any longer. "In the beginning, my work was exciting. I moved around a lot, so there was never time to dwell on anything but work. Then the opportunity in Montana came along, and I took it, thinking I would be happy."

"Permanence," he said. "Willy thought you'd decided it was time to settle down."

Her gaze snapped back to his. Had Willy also told him about her suddenly feeling incomplete? Needing more than just work? A life outside her career? A family? She wanted to be annoyed, but she loved Willy too much to care what he'd allowed to slip. Whatever he said to Huck, it was only because he loved Huck too and still harbored a deep-seated hope that the two of them would end up together eventually.

"Lots of people feel that way at my age." She shrugged, blowing off the notion. "The isn't-there-supposed-to-be-more syndrome." For her, it had started right after her twenty-ninth birthday. Suddenly all she could think about was the plans she and Huck had made when they were just silly kids. College first, get married. Travel the world and then settle down to begin a family at thirty. Here they were, thirty and thirty-one. Where was the more?

The memories tugged at her already raw emotions.

Fool.

"We had big plans for our thirties," he said. The way he said the words or maybe the words themselves had her struggling to breathe. "That was a very long time ago."

He reached out. She froze. His fingers brushed her cheek, tucked a loose strand of hair behind her ear. The touch had her heart moving too fast.

"It was." His hand fell away. "But it was real. I haven't felt anything real since…"

"Huck." She somehow managed to look him in the eyes. "We had a classic childhood love story. It was wonderful. The problem is we were kids. It wasn't meant to last because we had no idea what we really wanted."

For a moment, she thought he might argue with her point. Instead, he just turned away. "I'll lock up."

Had he seen that lie?

Because the truth was the last thing she remembered really wanting was him.

Chapter Seven

Huck had already brewed coffee when Olivia made an appearance. He'd heard her get up a while ago. She'd taken a shower, then gone back to her room for a while. At that point, he'd decided his need for food wouldn't wait any longer. He'd prowled through the fridge and the cabinets and come up with cheese toast. Thankfully, with diligent monitoring, he'd managed not to burn it.

"Good morning." She only glanced at him on her way to the coffee pot.

She'd hardly slept last night. He'd heard her puttering around in her grandparents' bedroom off and on all night. Even when he managed to doze off, the slightest sound had his eyes snapping open.

"Morning." He gestured to the table where

he'd arranged the cheese toast on two paper plates. "I figured I'd play it safe this morning."

She glanced at the stove, grimaced. "I'll need a few minutes to work up an appetite."

He laughed, couldn't help himself. "I'm still waiting on mine to show up."

She sat down at the table. "I hope you slept better than I did."

He pulled out a chair and joined her. "It's hard to keep watch and sleep at the same time." No need to mention he'd heard her every movement.

"It was hard to sleep in there around all their things," she confessed. "Harder than I expected."

"Guess so." She'd pulled her hair into a ponytail, the way she had when they were kids. She'd worn it that way the past couple of days. He liked it. Wearing it like that made her look so damned young. His gaze drifted down to her tee. He grinned. "I remember that shirt."

Nirvana.

"I didn't have a lot of options since I didn't bring enough clothes. Luckily, I still had a few things in the closet." She laughed. "Do you remember when I came home with it? Willy wanted to know why I bought it?" She shrugged. "I told him because Callie Letterman had one. You remember Callie, the most popular girl in high school."

"I remember her. She's a cashier at the market on Gunbarrel Road. Married. Two kids. Her husband teaches science at the middle school over in Dread Hollow."

"Really?" Olivia frowned. "I thought she went to New York to be a model."

"I guess it didn't work out." He picked up a slice of cheese toast and took a bite. Not bad.

"Anyway," Olivia picked up the piece of toast from her plate. "Willy refused to allow me to wear the shirt until he introduced me to the band's music. He said it was just wrong to wear a band tee and not know who they were."

"I can see his point." Huck grinned. "I remember Willy liked them almost as much as I did."

Olivia nibbled at her toast. "I've been thinking about the message and the photos. Your idea that this stranger might be my father got me thinking. The man in the photos is older. His hair is kind of grayish. It could be him—Kasey Aldean, I mean."

Twenty-seven years older—that was how long he'd been gone. Huck knew what the bastard had done. Even as a kid he'd wondered who left their child like that.

Far too many people. As an adult and a

member of law enforcement, he knew this well. In Olivia's case, it hadn't been so relevant. She'd had Willy. He had always been like a father to her. But not everyone was so lucky.

"Did he ever try to contact you or Willy?" Huck asked. He figured not, but it was possible there had been contact during those years he was away in Miami.

"Not that I'm aware of." Olivia nibbled her toast then set it aside as if that tiny bite had been enough. "I suppose it's possible he contacted Willy at some point, and Willy refused to pass along the message. He felt very strongly about Kasey having left the way he did. I don't think he planned to forgive him."

She was right on that one. Willy would have wanted to protect her from the father who had ghosted her all those years ago. No explanation for his abandonment would have been good enough.

"I can see if he's in the system. If he's ever been arrested or fingerprinted for any reason, I might be able to locate him."

"With that note on the wall," Olivia offered, "I suppose he's the closest thing to a person of interest we have right now. I just can't imagine why he would bother."

"Maybe he got religion. Decided it was time to make amends." Huck turned his hands up.

"Or was looking for money, like we talked about."

Willy had lived a very frugal life the past couple of decades. Other than Olivia's college tuition, he likely saved most of his income from new work and royalties from older work. Huck had no idea what his savings was like, but he imagined it was sizable. Enough so to tempt someone who might feel he was owed something. After all, Kasey Aldean had left Willy his daughter. What was a daughter worth?

The idea made Huck sick. What kind of man saw his child as a negotiable asset?

"I appreciate anything you can do to find him." She reached for her coffee again. "Part of me hopes he can't be found. If he wasn't part of this, he may see Willy's death as his invitation to attempt getting to know me." She shook her head. "I don't want to know him."

Huck reached across the table and put his hand on hers. "If I find him, I'll make sure he knows that."

She managed a wobbly smile. "Thanks."

The vibration of his cell warned he had an incoming text. He checked the screen. "They're releasing the—Willy." He typed a quick response. "I asked that they send him to the funeral home. The one that took care of your grandmother."

"Thanks. I'll call Mr. Nelson and let him know Willy requested cremation."

Huck remembered the service for Willy's wife. There hadn't been a coffin since she'd chosen cremation. The service had been held at Sunset Rock. Only close family and friends had been present. Willy and Olivia had scattered her ashes in the air. It was the sort of thing that made an impression on a ten-year-old boy.

"Are you planning a service?" With all that had happened, he hadn't had the opportunity to ask her.

She moved her head side to side, sadness shadowing her expression. "He made it very clear ages ago that he didn't want any sort of service. He just wanted his ashes spread at Sunset Rock. The same way we did Gran's except without all the fanfare."

That was Willy. He felt he'd had more than his share of notoriety with his photographs. He had preferred low-key these past few years.

Olivia looked to Huck. "I hope you'll be there with me. Willy would want you there."

"Of course."

A rap on the door had Huck pushing back his chair. "I'll see who it is."

OLIVIA STOOD, sending her own chair sliding back. Had the crime-scene investigators returned to search for more evidence? Maybe they had returned with news. She watched as Huck checked out the window.

"It's Ms. Lockhart, Madeline, from the diner."

Olivia remembered Ms. Lockhart. She'd always given Olivia the largest slice of pie in the case whenever she stopped in after school. Olivia had been certain the lady thought she and Huck were special since whenever they were at the diner she spent more time with them than any of her other customers. As Olivia had gotten older, she had realized the lady had a crush on Willy. He never seemed to notice, but Olivia had seen it every time they stopped at the diner. Olivia started toward the door and Huck.

"Morning, Ms. Lockhart," Huck said as he opened the door.

"Good morning, Huck." She beamed a smile. "How's your momma?"

"She's doing great," Huck said. "She and her sister have decided to start traveling the world. They're on a cruise right now."

"That's just wonderful." The lady stepped inside, a nine-by-eleven glass dish covered with aluminum foil in her hand. Her attention shifted to Olivia. "Oh, sweetie, I'm so sorry about Willy."

Olivia accepted her one-armed hug. No matter that she'd cried a dozen times already, emotion welled in her eyes and throat. "I'm still struggling with believing it."

How did you come to terms with the loss of the one person who had always been there?

The older woman drew back. "I brought that casserole you always loved." She offered the covered dish to Olivia. "The one with the chicken and the noodles and cheese."

Olivia smiled. It was still her favorite. Whenever she'd been in the field all week with work, she made this casserole when she came home and ate it the entire weekend. "Thank you. I could never make it the way you do, though I've tried so many times."

Sadness cluttered Madeline's face. "Do you know when you'll be spreading his ashes? He told me that's what he wanted, and I'd really love to be there."

All the times this lady had flashed her brightest smile for Willy from behind the counter at the diner flickered one after the other through Olivia's mind. Had he finally taken notice? It sounded as if they'd grown closer considering he'd shared his final wishes with her. "I would love for you to be there. We'll try for tomorrow. I'll let you know the time for sure."

"Thank you." She glanced from Olivia to Huck. "I should go. I'm sure you're busy."

"Ms. Lockhart," Olivia said, waylaying her

departure, "did Willy mention any trouble recently? Maybe someone who had visited him and upset him somehow?"

Her face paled. "Why, my gracious, no. He…" Her mouth slowly closed as if something besides what she'd intended to say had occurred to her. "He didn't mention anything, but I do believe something was bothering him."

"Would you like to join us for coffee?" Huck asked with a gesture toward the kitchen table.

"I would, but you know I have to get to the diner." She laughed. "Keep my staff on their toes."

The lady had owned the only diner in Sunset Cove for as long as Olivia could remember. "Something was bothering him?" Olivia prodded. "In what way?"

Madeline shrugged. "You know, as I so often say, the old gray mare ain't what she used to be, meaning at the end of the day I'm ready to collapse on the sofa and just relax. Willy…" She blinked, seemed to consider her words. "Some nights, we would relax at my house." She shrugged, her cheeks going pink. "Dinner and television. Other times, we'd come here."

Olivia smiled, her heart lifting at the idea. "I'm so glad to hear he was spending time with you and not here all alone."

Madeline visibly relaxed. "We enjoyed our

time together." A frown furrowed her brow. "Last week was like any other until Sunday. On Sunday…he seemed distracted. I had this sense of him being someplace else, so to speak. When I asked, he pretended not to know what I meant."

"He didn't mention anyone or thing?" Huck pressed. "Maybe something that didn't seem so important at the time."

Madeline looked from Huck to Olivia and back. "What's going on, Huck? Are you suggesting Willy's fall was no accident?"

"Do you believe it was?" Olivia asked, her tone more pointed than she'd intended. "If you spent a good deal of time with him, did you notice his balance being off or some issue that might have made him less sure-footed than usual?"

Her shoulders slumped. "I did. I spent all the time with him I could and the answer is no." Madeline closed her eyes and drew in a deep breath. "When Decker told me he'd fallen… that way, I didn't believe him. Then when the medical examiner didn't find anything, I tried not to think about it anymore."

Olivia reached out, put a hand on her arm. "Whatever happened, we're going to get to the bottom of it."

"You have my word on that," Huck promised.

A tear slipped down Madeline's cheek, and she swiped it away. "As much as I know in my heart he wouldn't have gotten that close to the edge if he didn't feel safe, I hope the other possibility isn't true. Willy didn't deserve to die that way."

Olivia bit her lip in an attempt to hold back her own tears. "When was..." She cleared her throat and started again. "When was the last time you saw his camera?"

Madeline made a face. "The camera? The one he always had with him?"

Olivia nodded. "We can't find it. Not where he fell and not here."

"We were together on Sunday. We went downtown for lunch. He had his camera then."

"Where downtown?" Huck asked the question that pounded in Olivia's brain.

"We went to Big River Grille on Broad. We both love—loved that place."

Olivia and Huck exchanged a look. "Did you go anywhere else downtown after that?"

She shook her head. "Like I said, he seemed very distracted. Said he didn't feel well." She shrugged. "The Cajun fish tacos weren't sitting right with him, so we went home early. We were back at my place by two and he begged off dinner that evening." Her gaze grew distant as if she were remembering that day. "I watched from the window as he left—the way I always do. But he didn't turn toward home."

"He went back toward the city," Huck guessed.

"Yes." Her arms went around herself as if she suddenly felt cold. "I told myself he just took a different way home, but I'm sure that wasn't the case."

Olivia passed the casserole to Huck and hugged the woman. "Thank you for telling me this." Olivia drew back. "It's really important that we understand how Willy was feeling and anyone he might have spoken to those last few days."

Madeline nodded. "You be careful." She looked to Huck. "If someone did this to Willy, he might still be around."

"Show her the picture," Huck said to Olivia.

She hadn't even thought of the pictures. She went back to the table and grabbed her cell. She showed the photos to Madeline. "These were on the dry rack in Willy's darkroom. Other than what's in his camera—if anything—I'm assuming these are the last photos he shot."

Madeline studied each photograph, then swiped to the next one. She shook her head. "I can't see him very well, so I can't say that I recognize him or the place." Her frown deepened. "Are you certain Willy took these photos? I've never seen him do such a poor job of focusing in on his subject." She handed the phone back to Olivia. "Maybe he was aiming for something else."

Olivia thanked Madeline again and Huck walked her to her car. Olivia returned to the kitchen counter where the original photos sat in a stack of other papers that hadn't really given them anything to go on just yet. She went through the photographs, one at a time, searching for any other detail that might have been what Willy was actually looking at when he took the shot. Something that he'd zeroed in on. All six were different, confirming to some degree that Willy had been following the man as he moved from outside the bar to inside and then when he came back out again, presumably later.

The man had to be the subject, but Madeline was right, this looked nothing like Willy's work. At first, Olivia had been so overwhelmed she hadn't even considered that aspect. Of course, she'd noticed the out-of-focus work, but she hadn't really considered it. And yet, the idea made complete sense.

This was not Willy's work. He hadn't taken these shots.

"Did you find something?"

Olivia looked up. She hadn't heard Huck

come back in. "She's right. Willy didn't do this."

Huck nodded slowly. "All right then, let's consider our timeline. Ms. Lockhart says she and Willy had lunch on Sunday. They were back at her place by two, and he left. She thinks he didn't go home." Huck's expression shifted to one of astonishment. "Wait. I saw Willy on Sunday." He popped his forehead with the heel of his hand. "It didn't cross my mind until Madeline said lunch on Sunday was the last time she saw him. I ran into him at the market around three-ish, maybe four. I was going in, and he was coming out."

"His camera was with him at lunch," Olivia noted. "She saw the camera. Did you see it later when you ran into him?"

"No." Huck shrugged. "But he'd been in the market. He probably left it in the Defender."

Olivia nodded. "Probably. Did he buy anything? I only ask because the fridge is basically bare. There was some cheese and a carton of expired milk but not much else."

Huck thought about the cheese toast he'd made. He'd used the only two slices of bread left in the house. "He only had one bag." He searched his memory for the image of Willy at the market that day. "There was one of those loaves of French bread. You know the kind that's always in baskets in random places so people will grab it as they go by."

Olivia nodded. "Like a baguette."

"Yeah, that's the one. Like when you're making spaghetti dinner. I saw one of those poking out of the bag and…a bottle of wine."

"Wait." She looked taken aback by that last one. "Willy never drank wine."

Huck shrugged. "Maybe it was for Madeline Lockhart."

Like him, Olivia stared at the door Ms. Lockhart had only just exited. "We'll have to ask her."

Huck nodded. "Back to the timeline. Willy was found around two on Monday afternoon. Sheriff Decker took the call himself."

"Those photos were taken at night," Olivia said, wanting to move past that horrible part in the story. "Since we know Willy had the camera Sunday as late as two, and if he didn't take those shots, then whoever killed him did. On Monday night, I'm thinking. Came here and developed the film without fear since Willy was gone and I hadn't arrived yet."

"Since his death was considered an accident," Huck went on, "there was no reason for anyone to come here to check things out. Decker knew to call you. No need to come here looking for contact info on next of kin.

But what if the wine was for our unsub? Maybe he came to dinner on Sunday night? We know it wasn't Ms. Lockhart or any of Willy's other friends I interviewed."

"Oh, my God, you're right." Olivia looked around. "At some point after three or four and maybe after dinner on Sunday night, the unsub, as you call him, was here. Did he have dinner with Willy? Did he leave and then come back later and search the house?"

"Which means," Huck realized, "the murder happened sometime after four on Sunday. And if our unsub wasn't Willy's dinner guest, he came later that night or on Monday night and searched the house. Even dared to come back while you were away yesterday and leave a message." Huck nodded, pieces falling into place. "You were right when you suggested he has a key."

Olivia's breath caught. "Where is Willy's key ring? We can confirm the key is missing if we find it. There would have been a key to the house, the shed. Everything."

Huck ran his hand through his hair, his mind—like hers—working to figure out the missing details. "Decker said the Defender was in the parking lot at the Point—where Willy always parked—so Decker drove it home the same afternoon—on Monday—when Willy was found."

He gestured to the door. "I'm guessing he left the keys in the vehicle."

Olivia was at the door by the time Huck caught up with her. She hurried to the Defender, opened the door. The heavy bundle of keys still hung from the ignition. A quick look confirmed the house, the shed and darkroom keys were missing.

"He took the keys after he killed Willy," she murmured. Her knees buckled.

Huck's arms went around her and pulled her against him. "We'll get him, Liv."

For a long minute, she allowed him to comfort her. But then she pulled free. "We should go back to that bar and talk to anyone we can find along that block. Maybe someone else saw Willy or the guy he was watching."

He had been thinking the same thing. "It's a long shot, but it's the best one we've got just now."

She nodded. "I'll get my bag."

Rick's Bar and Grill, Chattanooga,
10:30 a.m.

THE BAR WASN'T OPEN, but that didn't matter since it wasn't their destination this morning. The street was empty around it, making for good parking. Olivia climbed out of the SUV and walked around the hood to meet Huck.

"Where should we start?" Both sides of the street were lined with businesses. Several were closed down, the windows boarded up. Others were closed until after five.

"We'll start with the nail salon just over there." He nodded to her right. "Then go around the block."

"Should we split up?" She counted seven shops that appeared to be open.

"No way. We stick together."

Somehow she had known that would be his answer.

When they reached the nail salon, Olivia fell back a step and let Huck do the talking since the two female employees studied him closely from the moment he opened the door. Understandable, Olivia admitted. Huck was a good-looking man. Tall, fit, handsome.

She banished the thoughts, pretended to check out the nail polish colors while he chatted with the ladies. Neither had seen the blurry guy in the photos or Willy. Since this shop closed around the time the bar's clientele likely started to filter in, Olivia wasn't really surprised.

The next business, a print shop, had the same answer. Not open past five, hadn't seen either man.

"To tell you the truth," the print shop owner

admitted, "I don't come down here after dark. It's not safe."

The thought of Willy coming to a place like this had Olivia's nerves on edge. Willy had been in plenty of dangerous places in his life, but the danger had always been from the elements or the terrain. Never from another human.

It didn't make sense. Not coming here, not the blurry photos. She was certain Willy didn't do either of those things.

On the sidewalk, Olivia glanced back down the street at the bar. "Why would this person— this unsub—come here? Why take those shots and develop them?" Olivia wondered out loud. "Then leave them for me to find."

I knew you'd come back.

"If the goal was to leave me a puzzle to solve," Olivia grumbled, "I'm going to need a few more pieces."

"The message left on your bedroom wall," Huck said as they continued walking, "suggests Willy told whoever our unsub is that you wouldn't be coming back. He'd hidden your contact info from the bastard."

Olivia stalled, her heart bolting into a frantic rhythm. "Do you think he killed Willy because Willy wouldn't tell him where I was?" The idea had her stomach dropping to her feet.

The pain on Huck's face gave her the answer without him having to say a word.

"Oh, God." She started walking again. Had to move or risk falling into a heap of emotions that were already shattering into bits inside her.

"We can't be sure, Liv."

There he went speaking softly to her again. She wanted to scream. To hear him shout. This was wrong, wrong, wrong.

Breathe.

By the time they reached the final shop on their side of the street, she had calmed herself to a reasonable degree.

The shop was a small market that wrapped around the corner of the block. Inside was cold. Olivia shivered after walking the block in the heat. Today was a good deal warmer than yesterday, or maybe it was just the humidity. The woman behind the counter was older, closer to seventy than sixty, Olivia guessed.

Again, she hung back, allowed Huck to do the talking. Mostly because she didn't trust her emotions just now.

Huck provided the usual spiel and showed the photos he'd added to his phone as well. The woman put on her glasses and took her time, peering closely at each pic. When she finished, she shook her head.

Olivia wandered to the wide plate-glass window and found a spot between the signs spouting one sale or the other to peer out at the street. Was it possible her father had come back after all this time? Had he carried a grudge against Willy for some reason? Maybe he'd been in prison and only recently was released, like Huck suggested. Maybe there was some terrible secret about her father that Willy hadn't wanted to tell her.

"Thank you," Huck said, drawing Olivia's attention back to him. She walked toward him when he passed the woman a card as he had the other folks they had questioned today. "If you think of anything later, I hope you'll give me a call. We would be grateful for any help at all."

The woman had stopped listening to Huck and was staring at Olivia. When Olivia stopped next to Huck, the woman said, "Are you with him?"

Olivia looked to Huck then said, "Yes."

The woman frowned, then shook her head. "You look so familiar." She snapped her fingers, a light coming on in her eyes. "Wait, wait, wait. I know why you look familiar. There was a guy in here looking for you."

Adrenaline fired in Olivia's veins. "When was this?"

The woman shrugged. "Maybe Tuesday. I

can't say for sure. But he had a picture of you." Her gaze narrowed. "He just kept pushing me. Said you'd been seen in this area."

Olivia looked to Huck. "I've never been here before."

The woman set her hands on her hips. "Well, he sure thought you had."

"Are you certain the man who talked to you wasn't the one in the photo?" Huck asked.

She held out her hand. "Let me see those photos again."

Huck turned his phone over to the lady. She looked at the images for a long moment, then nodded. "I can't positively say so," she admitted as she handed the phone back to him. "But he's the right size, kind of skinny, and the height is right. And the fella asking about her did have grayish hair like the one in the blurry photos. Not the other one you showed me. It definitely wasn't him."

So not Willy, Olivia understood. The man in the photos outside the bar had come into this shop searching for someone who looked like Olivia. This was insane.

"The shoes or any of the clothing look familiar?" Huck asked, prompting her to look closer.

She shook her head. "Nah, but it could be him. For sure."

"What about his eyes," Olivia ventured. "Did you notice the color of his eyes?"

Her face scrunched up in thought. "I just can't remember. Not dark. Something lighter, but I can't say blue or gray or maybe hazel."

"He didn't leave you a card? A phone number or anything?"

The older woman frowned. "Wait just a minute." She went to the cash register, surveyed the bulletin board hanging on the wall next to it. She snatched a card from the board. "This is the one." She walked back to where they waited. "There's no name, but there is a phone number."

Huck accepted the card and immediately called the number. Olivia and the lady behind the counter watched and waited. Huck shook his head and ended the call. "Voice mail."

The lady shrugged. "Sorry but that's what he gave me."

"Thank you," Huck said again. "You've been very helpful."

As they walked toward the exit, the lady called after them, "Wait, wait, wait…"

Olivia and Huck turned back to face her once more.

"I remember something else. Something he said when he gave me that card."

Olivia held her breath, hoped it was a name…
anything useful.

"He said," she went on, "if I saw you I should
call that number or the police immediately
'cause you're *dangerous*."

Chapter Eight

Firefly Lane, 1:30 p.m.

Huck had called the number again. Finally, he left a voice mail.

He and Olivia had stopped at Nelson's Funeral Home to take care of the arrangements for Willy. His ashes would be ready when Nelson's opened tomorrow morning. Olivia had asked Huck to call Ms. Lockhart and the sheriff. He'd done so on the drive back to Willy's house. Both would be there. Then Decker had asked Huck for an update.

There wasn't a lot to say just yet, but the information the woman at the corner market had given basically confirmed what the message on her bedroom wall suggested: someone had been looking for Olivia. This unknown person could certainly be the person involved with Willy's death and the ransacking of his home and workspace.

So far, they hadn't talked much about the other part of what the woman had said. Olivia wasn't dangerous, and she certainly hadn't been in that neighborhood. She hadn't even been back in the state since Christmas.

Huck parked behind Olivia's SUV. He turned to her. She hadn't moved. Just sat in the passenger seat staring forward. He understood that focusing on Willy's arrangements had helped her to get past the woman's bizarre comments for a little while, but now there was nothing to do except examine the information more closely.

"I have a friend in Miami," Huck said.

Olivia turned to him and waited for the rest.

"He's not a cop, but he used to be one. He's a PI now, and he has the kind of contacts cops aren't supposed to use. I think he'll be able to help us figure out who this number belongs to."

She nodded. "I appreciate whatever you can do."

"Meanwhile," he suggested, "how about we look through your mother's things again and see if we find out anything else about your father?"

"You read my mind." She reached for her door.

Huck got out and met her on the stone path that led to the front porch. The sun was scorching today. Above average heat for June. Life in the South, he mused.

"You know," Olivia said, "when the waitress

said the guy had been looking for someone who looked like me, I thought she might be playing us." She shrugged. "But now…" She hesitated at the front door. "I just don't see how this is possible."

"It'll take time," he assured her, "but we will put the pieces together."

She exhaled a big breath, nodded.

When she would have unlocked the door, he reached for the key. "Why don't I do that?"

Without argument, she placed it in his hand.

He opened the door and took a step over the threshold. Fortunately, all looked exactly as they'd left it that morning.

"It's clear," he said, pulling the door open wider for her.

Still gun-shy, she walked in and looked around before visibly relaxing.

He closed and locked the door. "I'll do a walk-through, then, if you'd like, you can start looking through your mother's room while I make that call to my friend." He drummed up a smile. "I could warm up that casserole Ms. Lockhart dropped off. We should eat. We can't operate on adrenaline alone."

"Okay." The smile she managed was dim, but he appreciated the effort.

Olivia wasn't one to give up; he couldn't see her doing that now. She needed to be strong more than ever before, and he didn't doubt one little bit that she would do just that.

Huck did a quick walk-through, found no indication anyone had been in the house. Olivia disappeared into her parents' bedroom, and he made the call to Dex Trainor in Miami.

"Monroe," his old friend said, "I can't believe you haven't come running back by now. There must be more to that mountain than you shared."

Huck grinned. "It's home," he said. "We all know there's no place like home."

It had taken him ten years to understand that old saying was far too true.

"What can I do for you?" Dex asked.

"I have a cell number. I need to know who the number belongs to."

"Easy peasy," Dex said. "Give me the number, and I'll see what I can find."

Huck passed along the digits and thanked his old friend. They talked a minute more, with Dex giving him the lowdown on Huck's former colleagues. Huck appreciated they were all doing well, but that life was behind him now. He wasn't looking back any more than he was going back.

Huck warmed up the casserole and set the table, then he went in search of Olivia. She sat on the floor cross-legged, looking through old letters.

Huck sat down beside her. "What'd you find?"

She gestured to the pile of letters that sat in what looked like a scarf that had the wrinkles to show it had been tied around the bundle of letters. "I found these in the bottom drawer of Gran's dresser. Letters my mother had written to her when she was away with my father."

Huck picked up one of the letters and studied the graceful handwriting. "She signed with *X*'s and *O*'s."

"And little hearts." Olivia pointed to the hearts her mother had drawn along the bottom of her signature.

"You were just a toddler, basically, when she died." Huck passed the letter back to her. "Do you ever recall your gran or Willy mentioning any issues with your mom? Anger issues or…" He shrugged, hated like hell to say the other. "Or maybe mental health issues?"

Olivia shook her head. "Everything they ever said about my mother was positive. She was beautiful. She was happy. She gave them a great deal of joy. She loved me."

Huck considered the words used. "Never that she was a good mom or about her aspirations for what she wanted to do in the future?"

A frown worked its way across Olivia's face,

and he wanted so badly to trace it with his fingertips and then smooth it away.

"They never used those specific words," she said. "I can't say that I recall ever hearing about any plans she had for the future or anything that she specifically did with me or with them." She looked up at Huck. "Do you think there was some sort of issue? Maybe she didn't die of pneumonia. Maybe she died of a drug overdose, and that's why they've always been so closed up about it."

"We could see if there was a report done by the medical examiner's office. Or check with Mr. Nelson to see if he took care of your mother for the funeral."

"Better yet, you could talk to your mother." Olivia set the letters aside. "She might know things that she's never wanted to say to avoid hurting my feelings."

Huck pushed to his feet and held a hand out to her. "Come on. Lunch is ready. I'll call my mom while we eat."

Olivia took his hand and got to her feet. "Thanks."

He followed her to the kitchen, his stomach reminding him that he was beyond starved.

"Smells good." Olivia inhaled deeply. "And I'm actually hungry."

"That makes two of us."

While she poured glasses of ice water, Huck dished up the casserole. He waited until they'd settled around the table and Olivia had dug in before making the call. He put his phone on speaker and placed it on the table.

"Huck, what a lovely surprise," his mom said in greeting. "You just caught us. We're back in New Orleans, and we'll be heading to Tennessee on Sunday."

"I hope you had a good time."

"We did, but we're tired. Glad I don't have to drive home."

"Mom, I've got you on speaker, and Olivia is with me."

"Olivia." She fell silent for a moment then launched into her regrets for the loss of Willy. Olivia swiped at her eyes but kept a smile in place at his mother's enduring words.

"Thank you, Mrs. Monroe. I'm very grateful that Huck is with me."

Wow. He hadn't expected to hear those words in this lifetime.

"I would certainly be there as well if we hadn't been in the middle of the ocean when I heard the news. I am so sorry I can't be there."

"You're here in spirit," Olivia said, "and that's what matters."

"We have some questions for you," he said to his mother.

"All right," she said. "We're resting in our rooms until dinner, so fire away."

He smiled. "I'll let Liv do the asking." He looked to her to continue.

She placed her fork on the table and squared her shoulders. "I don't really remember my mom, and I'm certain everything Gran and Willy told me about her was biased. It would be, of course. Can you tell me if there were problems? Did Mom have any issues?"

Silence strummed in the air for a few seconds. Huck braced for whatever was coming. Olivia did the same, her shoulders visibly tensing.

"Your mother," she began, "was a beautiful child and an even more beautiful woman. You take after her in that way."

"Thank you. That's very kind of you to say."

Huck wanted to tell Olivia that anyone who wasn't blind would say the same thing. It wasn't about kindness; it was just the truth.

"When she met your father. Kasey. She fell head over heels in love. She was away in college and, I'm sure you know, that's where they met."

"My grandparents didn't know him at all, right?"

"That's correct. But when Laura came home with him, she was already expecting you, and your grandparents, though disappointed as you can imagine, welcomed them both. They adapted and went on with life. It was their way. Willy had a more difficult time, I think, but Joyce never missed a beat."

"I was aware of most of this," Olivia said. "I was born a few months later."

"Yes," Huck's mom continued. "In the beginning, I was convinced that everything was working out. Willy and Joyce seemed so happy. It was more difficult to tell about Kasey. I always got a sense of deception from him. And he was gone so much. By the time you were six months old, your mother would disappear with him for a week or two. Sometimes he would stay gone for more than a month."

"Disappear?" Olivia looked to Huck. "I know they traveled a lot. For my father's work, I assumed."

Another few moments of silence. "I hate telling you this," she said, "if Joyce and Willy had chosen not to."

"Please," Olivia said, "I need to know the truth."

"It's important, Mom," Huck confirmed. "There are some things happening here that we need to better understand."

"Should I be worried?" she asked, always concerned for her son even though he was a grown man.

"I'm fine," he assured her. "It's not about me. It's about the past."

"Okay." Though she sounded skeptical, she continued. "There were many times when your grandparents had no idea where your mother was. She and Kasey would just disappear without telling anyone. If it involved any sort of work, I was never told. Worse, when Laura was home, she wasn't herself. I wasn't privy to all the details but what I do know is that Willy and Joyce worried all the time. Joyce was terrified that the next time your parents disappeared, they might take you away too. Thank God that never happened."

OLIVIA FELT GOBSMACKED. Why had Willy never told her about their fears? She could understand her gran never saying anything, Olivia had still been a child when she died. But Willy should have told her at some point.

"Did Willy or Gran ever say why they thought my mother behaved this way?" Olivia almost wanted to stop this conversation right now. It turned all that she'd believed about her mother upside down.

"Willy was convinced something happened to Laura during her first year of college. Maybe the stress was too great. It's possible she dabbled in drugs, though there was never any confirmation of this. But it was like when she came back from college after dropping out, she was a different person. There were moments when we would see the old Laura, but those were few and far between. She was short-tempered and…and violent even."

"Violent?" Olivia felt ill. She hadn't expected this complete about-face from what she had been led to believe.

"Kasey would show up with bruises and black eyes. Several times, Laura broke things. But it wasn't like that all the time, Liv. There was something wrong, I'm certain. It doesn't seem that way since she was home for parts of four years before…." She paused for a moment. "But the problems slowly escalated, and with the long absences, Willy and Joyce didn't understand just how bad it was. Kasey took off, and then, well, you know. Laura passed."

Reeling, Olivia had to ask. "Did she really die of pneumonia?" In light of all she'd just learned, Olivia no longer trusted what she'd been told. Clearly, her grandparents had wanted to protect her, but this was a lot to keep from her.

"The truth is," Mrs. Monroe said softly, "I don't know how she died, but it wasn't pneumonia."

"Christ," Huck muttered. "Why didn't you tell me this?"

Olivia shook her head. "Huck, don't go there."

"I made a promise," his mother said. "Willy asked me, for Joyce's sake, never to speak of it and never to tell a soul. I promised I wouldn't, and until just this moment, I have not."

Olivia nodded, her emotions whirling way too fast. "I understand, and I truly appreciate you telling me now. It's important that I know."

"Liv's right," Huck said. "Thank you for telling us. I know it was difficult for you to under the circumstances."

"You know," his mother went on, "your father and I were very old when we had you, Huck. We loved Laura. Willy and Joyce were so kind to allow us to enjoy her childhood as if she were part of our family too. Then, when Laura went off to school, I found out I was expecting you. It was the greatest blessing. We were very, very lucky. But sometimes things go wrong for reasons we can't understand. Joyce and Willy had to face that awful unknown, and I know they were able to face it with far less difficulty because of you, Liv. You gave them the strength and courage to carry on. Always remember that."

"Thank you." Olivia wasn't sure she could stay still any longer. She stood.

"Thanks, Mom," Huck said. "We'll talk again soon."

"Okay. I'll see you soon. Love to both of you."

Olivia was on her way to the back door before the call ended. She needed air. To walk off all these feelings.

Huck caught up with her outside. "I'm sorry, Liv. I had no idea."

"Well, at least now we know why this guy—assuming he's my father—is going around asking people about me and saying I'm dangerous. I suppose he assumes since I look like my mother, I must be like my mother in other ways."

Huck put a hand on her shoulder, turned her around mid-step. "No, you are not like the woman my Mom just described. That wasn't even your mom. That was whatever demon had stolen her life. I know you, Liv. You are the kindest person on this planet. You would never purposely hurt anyone. And I'm certain your mother was the same, but something happened to change her. As sad as that is, it wasn't your fault, and it doesn't mean it has or will happen to you."

He'd read her mind. Though her mother had been younger when this breakdown or change happened to her, Olivia couldn't help thinking about all the times she had felt so stressed. But she'd never lost touch with who she was and turned into someone else. At least not to her knowledge. What if she didn't know? Could she have come back here without telling Willy and gone to that bar?

No, that wasn't possible. She was always at work. No way.

"You're right, I know." She managed a smile for Huck's benefit. "It's just tough to hear a truth like that when you thought you'd known the truth all along."

"Maybe it was a bad idea."

"No." She shook her head. "With all that's going on, it was necessary." She reached out and took his hand. "Walk with me."

His fingers curled around hers, and he followed as she moved forward. It wasn't until she was nearly to the cliffs that she understood where she was going. She spotted the big tree and the bench that stood beneath it. Joyce and planted flowers all around the tree's massive trunk for Laura.

Laura Ballard was buried beneath that big tree.

Olivia sat down on the bench Willy had built. There was no headstone. He'd carved her mother's name into the wood.

Huck held onto her hand and stood next to

her. She was glad. Despite their not-so-happy history, she was very glad he was here. She needed him maybe more than she ever had before. She stared at her mother's meticulously kept grave.

How was it that one person could leave behind so much damage?

Willy and Gran had been good people. They hadn't deserved that kind of tragic loss. But most who suffered tragedies didn't.

Olivia wondered whether things might have turned around if her father had stayed. If he had been here, maybe her mother would have managed to keep going.

If he was back, Olivia intended to find him. Maybe she would ask him why he hadn't tried harder for her and her mother's sakes.

If he had hurt Willy…well, she wasn't sure what she would do.

She squeezed Huck's hand. She hoped he would help her make the right choice.

Chapter Nine

Olivia stared at her reflection. The ivory dress fit her perfectly. The light tan pumps she'd found worked well with the dress and weren't so high-heeled. The image in the mirror shook her just a little.

Somewhere in all those photos, there was one of her mother wearing this dress. Olivia had seen it a thousand times.

The memory sent a chill racing over Olivia's skin.

Though Willy never really talked about her mother, Gran had spoken of her often. She had gone through the photos of Laura many times with Olivia and talked about the moments.

Olivia turned away from the mirror. She hadn't gotten up this morning with the idea that she would wear one of her mother's dresses—

there were dozens hanging in that closet—but she hadn't considered until then that she had nothing to wear this morning.

When she'd thrown those few things into her overnight bag, preparing for a memorial hadn't been on her mind. But then Willy wouldn't have cared if she'd worn jeans. But Olivia needed to dress up for this. It was the last time she would hold any part of him in her hands. There would be no more hugs, no more smiles from him.

This day had to be special. For him.

A soft rap on her door had her heading that way. It was time to go. Sheriff Decker was picking up Willy's ashes. He and his wife were bringing Madeline Lockhart along. Olivia felt confident their attendance would make Willy happy. Because whatever he thought, his life had been worth making a fuss over.

Olivia opened the door. Huck smiled at her. He looked nice this morning. The navy shirt brought out the paler blue of his eyes. She'd always loved staring into those striking eyes. The jeans were classic Huck. They'd driven to his house last night for him to pick up a few things. She'd made the mistake of following him to his room. The framed photo of them on his dresser had stolen her breath. It had been taken at Sunset Rock by Willy. It was the day before she left for college. When he'd noticed her staring at it, Huck had mentioned that the photo was his mom's favorite.

Olivia thought maybe it was his favorite too. There was a duplicate tucked away somewhere at her townhouse.

"You ready?"

She pulled herself back to the here and now. Smiled. "I am."

They walked out of the house, locking the door for the good it would do. Huck hustled ahead of her and opened the passenger-side door.

As she climbed in, he said, "You look great."

"Thanks." She gave him a nod. "You too."

His broad grin lightened the sadness just a little.

She settled into her seat as he rounded the hood then scooted behind the wheel. When he'd turned the SUV around and was headed away, she figured it was a good time to say what needed to be said.

"I know we've spent a lot of years apart."

He glanced at her, his eyes saying it all. The pain there matched her own.

"We both said and did things…"

"There are no words," he hastened to say when she hesitated, "to explain how much I regret my actions."

"Same here," she confessed. And why not? It was true. It was time to put the past behind them. "Your being here through all this means a great deal to me. I hope, moving forward, we can be friends."

He grinned at her. "I will always be here, Liv."

He didn't exactly agree to the friends part, but she thought maybe that was implied by his words.

How could they not be friends?

Definitely they could be friends.

Huck drove to one of the parking spaces higher up the mountain, closer to their destination. Good thing, considering the shoes she wore. They might not have such high heels, but they definitely weren't made for hiking. Another vehicle was already there.

"That's Decker's car," Huck said as they passed it on the way to the overlook.

Olivia's emotions had gotten the better of her as they approached Sunset Rock, the place Willy had loved so much. Sheriff Decker and his wife waited, the small recyclable box containing Willy's ashes in his hand. Ms. Lockhart stood by, her eyes red from crying. But it was the rose-colored dress that stood out. She looked beautiful. Olivia was glad all over again that she had been in Willy's life, even if he hadn't shared the news with Olivia. Everyone deserved to have someone.

The thought had her glancing at Huck. He deserved someone too. Was the relationship they shared so long ago holding him back?

Could she say it hadn't held her back?

The idea twisted the already tight emotions inside her.

"Olivia." Decker offered the box to her.

"I thought we could each say something and spread part of his ashes." Her lips trembled on the last part.

Okay, keep it together. She didn't want to fall apart until this was done.

Decker smiled. "Good idea."

"Would you go first?" Olivia asked.

"I will." The sheriff and his wife stepped forward.

Decker talked about how much he would miss his longtime friend and avid fishing buddy. He and his wife each reached into the box and removed a portion of ashes, then allowed them to flow through their fingers. After a moment of silence, they moved back a few steps and passed the box to Olivia.

"Ms. Lockhart," she said, holding the box toward the older woman.

Madeline nodded, tears dampening her

cheeks. She moved forward. "I'll miss you, Willy."

Olivia felt whatever else Lockhart had to say was most likely private and stepped back to give her a moment. When ashes had filtered from her fingers, she brought the box back to Olivia.

Olivia turned to Huck. "Will you do this with me?"

He nodded and walked to the edge with her. They had stood here so many times. They had loved this place just as Willy had.

For a long moment, Olivia couldn't speak. She stared out over the beauty that had captivated the man who had marveled at magnificent views all over this planet and yet always came back to this one. Huck opened the box and started first.

"Thank you for always being you, Willy." Ashes floated from his fingers. "Life won't be the same without you."

Olivia smiled, fighting a flood of tears. "I love you, Willy." Ashes slipped from her fingertips. "I'll try my best to make sure all your hopes and dreams for me come true."

More than anything else, he wanted her to be happy and fulfilled. She hoped she could make all that he wanted happen. She glanced at Huck. She'd suggested they stay friends; that was a good first step.

The five of them finished giving Willy the send-off he had requested. When they were back at the parking site and Mrs. Decker and Ms. Lockhart were in the sheriff's car, Decker followed Olivia and Huck to his SUV.

"I talked to the lead investigator of our CSI team this morning. They didn't find anything. None of the prints collected were in the system."

Huck shook his head. "I was afraid that would be the case."

Decker shrugged. "Just proves our guy is smarter than the average perp."

"I'm still working on finding the guy in the photos." Huck told his boss about the woman at the market they'd spoken to yesterday, but he didn't mention the phone number or the friend he'd called for help.

Olivia doubted the sheriff would want to know about any steps outside the usual protocol. If they were lucky, the friend would find something useful.

When the sheriff had driven away, she and Huck loaded into his vehicle. "What now?" she asked.

"Now we go back to the cabin so you can change those shoes."

She laughed, her heart still so heavy. "And the dress?"

He shot her a wink. "I kind of like the dress."

Olivia stared out the window as he drove toward home. *Home.* This would always be home. She had lived many other places, but none were engrained so deeply.

"Monroe."

Huck answering his cell had her turning toward him.

He listened for a while then said, "All right, man. Thanks. I owe you." The call ended, and he glanced at Olivia. "That was my friend from Miami. The number is registered to a burner phone."

Olivia frowned. "What does that mean exactly?" She had heard the term.

"It means someone bought the phone and the minutes without a contract. Probably paid cash so there's no way to connect the phone to him or her."

Not the news she had hoped for. "Great."

"Yeah," Huck agreed. "We'll just keep looking."

"Thanks."

He glanced at her. "You don't need to worry, Liv. Even if it wasn't my job, I wouldn't give up."

She wouldn't have expected anything else. As far as she knew, he'd only given up once.

She blinked the memory away. Reminded herself that whatever happened in the past, they could still be friends. She wasn't going back on that. Ever.

Firefly Lane, 11:30 a.m.

OLIVIA UNLOCKED THE door and walked in. The first thing she did was step out of her mother's shoes.

Huck's hand on her arm made her stop and stare at him. He nodded toward something across the room. Her gaze followed his, and on the kitchen table, positioned right in the middle, was her grandfather's camera.

"Stay right here by the door," he ordered, "until I have a look around."

Olivia leaned against the closed door, needing the support, and watched as Huck drew his weapon. He kept it with him always but rarely wore it when it was just the two of them. This morning, he'd left it in his SUV for the memorial service. Ever vigilant, he'd brought it into the house when they arrived. Good thing, she decided.

When he'd completed a walk-through of the house, he gave her a nod.

She rushed across the room and reached for the camera but stopped just shy of touching it. She looked to Huck, who stood beside her now. "I should wait until we check for prints?"

He shrugged. "I don't see the point. He didn't leave them anywhere else, why change his MO now?"

Huck was right. Olivia picked up the camera. Checked for damage. Saw none. She frowned. "Someone took photos."

"He wants you to see," Huck suggested, his face heavy with worry. "He's playing with you."

Olivia squared her shoulders. "Let him play. He's not going to win."

Huck gave her a nod. "Damn straight he's not."

"I should change before we go to the dark-room." She certainly didn't want to damage her mother's dress with chemicals.

HUCK STRUGGLED TO hang on to patience.

It took some time to develop the film. In the darkroom, he watched each step from the moment Olivia removed the film from the camera and its cassette. He watched her ready the film and the tanks for what came next. She prepared the developer mixture. Checked the temperature and then poured it into the film tank. She moved through the steps as if she'd done this just yesterday. It wasn't until after the rinse and careful soak in wetting agent that she started to remove the film from the reel she'd used for the developing process.

She unrolled it, cut it into shorter strips and hung the strips to dry.

"It's him," she said, peering at several of the shots with Willy's loupe. "This time the shots are clear."

When she reached the final strip, she gasped. Huck tensed.

"I think it's the guy from the other photographs. He's dead. Shot." She straightened and passed the loupe to Huck. "At least, he looks dead. Maybe this is part of some sick game."

Huck viewed the film strips. Definitely the man from the photos, Huck decided. He was lying on the ground, two holes in his chest. Blood pooled around him. Either someone was very, very good at staging and theatrical makeup, or the guy was dead.

He studied the scene. The man appeared to be on a porch or patio. Huck moved back to the other shots. Whoever had taken the photographs had followed the victim for a while. The shot of him walking along a sidewalk had captured a street sign down the block.

"I think I know where he is." He placed the loupe on the table and turned to Olivia. "We need to find this guy."

"His body?" she countered.

Huck nodded. "Sure as hell looks that way."

Before leaving, Huck zoomed in and snapped photos of the shots he might need. The quality wasn't the best but since the strips had to finish drying before they could be used for creating actual photos, they would have to do.

After locking up the house—for the good it would do—they headed into Chattanooga.

"Why would he kill someone, take photos and leave them for us to find?"

Huck glanced at Olivia. She stared forward, her profile furrowed with worry. "Like I said, it's some sort of game."

"What kind of person plays games with murder?"

This was the part he didn't really want to talk to her about. He could be wrong, but deep down he knew he wasn't.

"Usually when you're dealing with a killer who likes to play games, it's someone who has done it before."

"Are you saying he could be a serial killer?"

The horror in her voice had his fingers tightening on the steering wheel.

"No. I'm not saying that—I'm saying this isn't a first kill." He should consider his words more carefully, he decided. "At this point," he reminded her, "we don't know who caused

Willy's death any more than we do who killed the guy in the photos. Assuming he's dead."

And that was a pretty good assumption.

"But if your unsub is him—my father," she said, "you're saying the way this looks, he could be a repeat killer."

Not a question. She got it. All that crime TV, he mused.

But this wasn't TV. This was real life. *Her* life.

"Yes." He wasn't going to lie to her.

"What are the other options?" She twisted more fully in the seat. "There are others, aren't there?"

He slowed as they reached the city limits. "Yes, there are other possibilities."

"Like he could be deranged, mentally ill?"

"It's possible." He braked for a red light. "Remember, all of these are theories. We don't know anything yet."

She shifted forward again. "It's just hard to take considering I just learned my mother suffered from some sort of mental illness no one thought I should know about, and now my father appears to be a killer."

"You're not a killer and you are not mentally ill," he said, hoping to convey the certainty of his words with his eyes.

She looked away. "The light's green."

He shifted his attention back to driving. "Liv, you can't borrow trouble like this. You're already under a great deal of stress. You just lost Willy. Give yourself a break. You are not a bad person or a person with issues of any sort."

"How do you know?" she demanded, anger in her tone now. "You and I have been apart for a decade." She pounded her chest. "I could have been in and out of mental hospitals all this time for all you know."

"I know," he said, his eyes on the road and navigating the heavier traffic, "because Willy would have told me."

"He didn't tell me about my mom," she argued, the anger weakening now.

He glanced at her. "Because we talked about *you* all the time. I strong-armed him into an update after every conversation he had with you."

"Why?"

Those three little letters were crammed full of emotion. The frustration he recognized. Impatience. And something else that sounded far too much like hurt. Damn it. He hadn't meant to hurt her. He'd been young and stupid, and he'd made a monumental mistake.

"Because I care." He hoped she would leave it at that.

"Why would you still care that much after all this time?"

No such luck.

"We're here," he said, avoiding the question. He pulled to the curb and shifted into Park.

She leaned forward, peered out at the street. "Oh, my God, you're right." She pointed to the street sign at the end of the block. She released her seatbelt. "What do we do now?"

He released his own. "We start with the houses that are empty. They'll be the easiest to access and offer the most likely place for where an unreported shooting could take place."

She surveyed both sides of the street. "Looks like most of the houses are unoccupied."

"That will work to our advantage."

They climbed out, met in front of his SUV. Only two other vehicles sat along the street. Both older, both appeared as if they had been there for a while.

"It looks as if the houses have been vacant for a long time," she said as she followed Huck along the cracked sidewalk to the first house on the left.

"There's about three streets in the area that are like this." Abandoned. Forgotten. "The good news," he said as he stopped at the steps up to the porch, "is people have started buying the houses a couple of streets over and turning them into nice homes. So maybe there's hope."

"Maybe." Olivia stared at the dilapidated house in front of them.

One by one, they checked the front and back yards of the houses, first one side of the street, then the other. In the photo, the man was lying on a porch or a patio—concrete. Old and cracked like the sidewalks leading to each one.

Since the street was a dead end, there was no traffic.

City sounds floated on the air from blocks away. The distant echo of traffic played a constant background to the other faraway sounds.

The fifth house from the last on the block proved to be the one they were looking for. The smell warned Huck before his gaze traced over the body.

"Stay here," he said to Olivia, indicating the rear corner of the house. "I can still see you if you stay here, but I can't have you getting any closer. This is a crime scene now."

She nodded her understanding.

He drew his weapon, though he doubted anyone, particularly the killer, was about. When he reached the crumbling patio, the victim lay on his back just as he had in the photos. Judging by the condition of the body, he'd been dead a day, maybe a day and a half.

Huck called Decker before calling the discovery in to Chattanooga PD. Since he didn't have gloves, checking for a wallet or any other type of ID would have to wait.

If this wasn't Liv's long-lost dad, who the hell was it?

Chapter Ten

2:50 p.m.

Huck's patience was wearing thin.

He and Olivia had been waiting for more than an hour. The detective on call had arrived half an hour ago, and still they had been told nothing.

He paced the sidewalk in front of the house—the crime scene. Olivia leaned against the driver-side door. She was obviously growing more anxious with every passing moment, but so far, she had remained calm.

If the dead guy was her long-lost father... damn, Huck couldn't even imagine how she would feel. Her father had been in his early twenties when he and Olivia's mother were together. Olivia wasn't sure of his exact age. Twenty-seven years later, he would be around fifty or so. The victim looked to be in that age range.

Huck paused, stared beyond the yellow tape

now draping the yard. All the activity was taking place behind the house, so he could see nothing.

"Maybe the detective forgot we're waiting," Olivia said.

Huck walked over to where she stood, propped against the side of his vehicle. "We're not a priority for him, that's for sure." And understandable. The man had a job to do. They'd given a statement to the first officers on the scene, but Huck expected there to be more questions from the detective.

"If that is my father," she ventured, her voice revealing her weariness, "I just don't get why he would be asking about me and calling me dangerous."

Huck had considered the same questions. "I'm thinking he exaggerated his story about you to get the desired reaction. People are more likely to make that call if they believe danger is involved."

He shifted his attention from the house to her. "The big questions in my mind are why look here or at that bar? Why would he think you would be in this area?"

A frown marred her smooth brow. "Maybe Willy told him to look here to throw him off track. He may have thought he was protecting me."

Which left one big, glaring question. "If this scenario is even remotely accurate, why not warn you?"

Olivia shook her head. "That's the part I can't make fit. Willy would never leave me hanging like this." Confusion deepened those frown lines. "Why didn't he go to Sheriff Decker and ask for help?"

"Or me," Huck pointed out. "I talked to him all the time. On Sunday, for God's sake...before what happened. Not a word was mentioned about trouble of any sort. He seemed just fine."

"Monroe."

Huck shifted his attention to the detective heading in their direction. *About time.* He straightened away from the vehicle. "Detective Kepler."

Kepler paused on the sidewalk next to where they waited and flipped through his little notebook. "Tell me again what brought you here."

Huck explained about Willy and the photos. He didn't go through the whole spiel about the missing camera that suddenly reappeared. That could wait for another time. He also didn't mention the lady in the corner market. Not relevant just yet.

"And you do not know this man, Ms. Ballard. Is that correct?"

"I do not," Olivia confirmed.

Huck was glad she left her answer at that. No need to mention their suspicions just yet.

"Well," Kepler turned to the next page, "let's remedy that right now. His name is Louis Rogers. He's a private investigator here in Chattanooga." He shrugged. "Low-rent sort. No criminal record. A few minor traffic violations but basically a clean guy."

"You're sure that's who he is?" Olivia pressed. "Could he be carrying a fake ID?"

Kepler shook his head. "I've run into him on cases before. I know him, or I should say I used to know him. We went to high school together a million years ago. Anyway, any ideas on why someone would send your grandfather photos of him? Or why your grandfather took photos of him?"

"I'm sorry, I have no idea. I only came back to town a few days ago because my grandfather died. Murdered, we think."

Kepler looked to Huck then. "You said the grandfather may have been murdered Sunday night or early Monday. I'm guessing this guy bought the farm a couple days ago, give or take. The ME is on the way, and we'll know more then."

"Anything in the house?" Huck asked. He'd

peeked in a few windows and didn't see anything. The place looked vacant.

"Nope. The houses on this block are all vacant. Rumor is they're all being taken down by some developer who has plans for one of those commercial housing developments."

Huck pulled a business card from his pocket. "Give me a call if you need anything else or find something that might be useful to my case."

Kepler tucked the card into his jacket pocket. "I hope you'll do the same."

"No question," Huck confirmed.

Kepler seemed satisfied with his answer and wandered back to his crime scene.

When he was out of hearing range, Olivia asked, "What now?"

"Now we go to Mr. Rogers's office before Kepler heads in that direction."

When they had settled into his SUV, she said, "Good plan."

"Let's just hope Mr. Rogers has an employee or kept good notes about his cases."

The medical examiner's van arrived as they were driving away, announcing to anyone in the vicinity that there was a body to be examined and removed.

Kepler wouldn't be going anywhere for a while.

Lee Highway, 4:00 p.m.

THE PI'S OFFICE was in a strip mall shoehorned between a now permanently closed candy store and a vacant office currently for lease.

When the detective had said low-rent, Olivia had anticipated something far sleazier. The area wasn't bad, and the offices, though old, appeared in good condition. They were in luck since a woman was in Rogers's office.

When Huck opened the door for Olivia, the woman looked up.

"We're closed," she announced. The swollen, red-rimmed eyes told Olivia she had heard the news.

Huck showed his badge. "Deputy Detective Monroe. This is my associate." He tilted his head in her direction. "We have a few questions for you, ma'am."

"You weren't supposed to be here for another hour or so," she said, clearly annoyed.

Based on the files spread haphazardly across her desk, Olivia decided the lady was hoping to get rid of any incriminating evidence before Detective Kepler arrived. Private investigators had a reputation for operating outside the law at times.

Huck held up his hands. "You have nothing to worry about from me," he assured her. "The detective who's coming next is the one who will be looking for the dirt. Also, I'm sorry for your loss, ma'am. My associate here just lost her grandfather—he was murdered too, and we need your help. That's why we're here. It's the only reason we're here."

She looked from Huck to Olivia. "Make it fast. I don't have a lot of time to tidy up."

"I understand," Huck confirmed. "Can you tell us what case your partner was currently working on?"

The woman collapsed into the chair behind her desk. "I'm—was—his assistant. He was working on a family issue related to a man named William Ballard."

Olivia's heart thumped against her ribcage. "That's my grandfather. He was murdered…"

The assistant closed her eyes and exhaled a big breath. "I was afraid of that." She opened her eyes once more and met Olivia's gaze. "I heard about Mr. Ballard's death, but there was no mention of murder." Another big breath. "Louis had been MIA since Wednesday morning. He got a phone call real early. We were both still asleep. He said he had to go, and he never came back."

So this lady was more than an assistant to Rogers. "Did you report him missing?"

She shook her head. "He told me never to do that unless he was MIA with no contact for seven days."

Olivia stepped closer, held out her hand. "I'm Olivia Ballard. I'm very sorry for your loss and even sorrier that it may have been connected to my family somehow."

The assistant stood, accepted Olivia's hand. "Gina West. Sorry for yours too."

"Can you tell us more about the case?" Huck asked.

Their hands fell apart, and Olivia held her breath, hoping for some information that would help answer the mounting questions about Willy's death. Her chest tightened at the idea that it looked more and more like it was related to her missing father.

"Mr. Ballard," Gina said, "wanted everything kept quiet. It was imperative to him that no one knew about whatever was happening. Louis never told me the details, and I never asked. When a client requests that level of confidentiality, I've learned it's best if I don't ask questions. Louis always told me what I needed to know and nothing more." She moved her head side to side. "I know basically nothing about the case, and Louis didn't write anything down."

Olivia's hopes plummeted. This could be just another dead end.

"You didn't overhear anything that might help us?" she asked.

"I'm sorry. No. Louis met with his client away from the office. It was all very secretive. I'm assuming he met with Mr. Ballard since he called it the Ballard case, but I never met or spoke to the client."

Another shake of her head. "I can tell you," she said, "that Louis may have used one or more of his sources for help with the case."

"Can you give us contact info?"

"Normally, I wouldn't…" She blinked rapidly to hold back the tears shining in her eyes. "But I guess it doesn't really matter at this point." She zeroed in on Huck. "If what you're looking for can somehow help find who killed Louis, I'm game."

Gina provided a list with three names and contact information. Those, she said, were the people her boss relied upon most often. She also promised to contact Huck if she learned anything relevant to the Ballard case.

As they drove away, all Olivia could think was that she never dreamed her family would become a murder case.

Huck insisted they stop for food while he attempted to reach out to the names on the list provided.

The diner he chose was an old one on Tremont Street in Chattanooga, but the atmosphere was casual and comfortable. The music wasn't too loud, and there wasn't much of a crowd.

Olivia picked at her sandwich. She told herself to eat, but it was difficult with all the emotions crowded into her throat.

The first two names on the list came with cell numbers. Huck's calls went unanswered, not entirely surprising, so he left voice mails with the promise of a reward for information. Hopefully that would prompt responses.

The third name had no contact number, but his employer's address was listed. A car wash only a few blocks away, which was the reason, she learned, Huck had chosen this diner.

"I just don't understand why he didn't tell me," Olivia said finally. She pushed her plate away. She hadn't been able to manage more than a bite or two. How could she? "This makes less and less sense. Willy and I always talked about everything. Why change now?"

Huck reached across the table and squeezed her hand. "He was protecting you. For me, the real question is why didn't he come to me for help?"

"Good question. I can only assume he thought he would be able to handle it on his own." She shrugged. "With the PI's help."

"Still doesn't make sense to me," Huck countered. "If he was going to anyone for help, why not me? I'm here. I'm a cop."

A sour taste rose in Olivia's throat. "Maybe because you're a cop."

Huck stared at her as if the idea had just struck him as well. "You're thinking that he didn't want me or you to know about whatever this is."

She nodded slowly, the concept settling fully. "Maybe my father is some sort of criminal, like you suggested, and he didn't want me to find out. He may have been concerned you would tell me."

Huck pulled out his wallet and left cash on the table for their food. "Let's see if we can find his guy at the car wash."

As they left the diner, Olivia considered that the spreading of Willy's ashes felt like a dream now though it had been only a few hours ago. She still found it difficult to comprehend that he would never come home again.

Had her mother felt that way after her father left? A completely different situation, of course, but the sense of emptiness must have been similar. Olivia couldn't help wondering if her work would ever be enough to fill this new void.

She glanced at the man behind the wheel as they drove away from the diner. At some point after he left ten years ago, she had convinced herself that she no longer missed him, but that had been a lie. She could see that now. Being here with him in light of all that was happening, it was easy to see just how badly she had missed him.

She looked away, stared out the window. What a mess they were. Pushing away the thought, she focused on the present. Finding the truth had to be priority one just now.

The car wash was busier than Olivia would have expected. Then again, she supposed everyone wanted their cars nice and clean for the weekend. In Montana, she rarely worried about her vehicle's appearance. Between the snow and the remote sites to which she was often assigned, keeping a vehicle clean was pointless.

"It might go more smoothly if you wait here. Keep the doors locked." He lifted the console lid and pulled his weapon out, placed it on the closed lid. "This won't take long."

Too mentally fatigued to question his decision, she agreed. "All right."

He climbed out, closed the door and waited

until she hit the lock button, then he went into the car-wash office. They had no idea what this source looked like or even if he was at work today.

Half a dozen men and women were busily wiping down freshly washed cars. When those vehicles were picked up by their owners, more pulled out of the car-wash tunnels to take their places, and the whole process started over again.

Huck exited the office and approached one of the men drying a vehicle. The man's body language shouted loudly and clearly of his wariness, but he didn't take off. Olivia felt her hopes rising. The longer the two talked, the more hopeful she became.

Her pulse jumped when Huck shook the man's hand and headed back to the SUV. Olivia hit the unlock button and mentally crossed her fingers.

Huck climbed in and shifted into Reverse. "It isn't much, but it's something. Rogers gave him an address to surveil. He was to let Rogers know if anyone went in or out of the house."

"Did he see anyone at the location?"

As he pulled out onto the street, Huck shook his head. "He did not. Maybe we'll have better luck."

Vine Street, 6:30 p.m.

HALF AN HOUR with no activity had elapsed since Huck parked across the street from the address Rogers's source had provided. A real-estate sign was in the yard listing the house for sale.

The house on the right of the property appeared to be empty. A for-rent sign stood in the yard. On the left, an older lady sat on the porch in a rocking chair, rocking and fanning herself with one of those old-fashioned hand fans once given out by churches. Huck's grandmother had been so proud of hers. She'd told him repeatedly that it was a blessing not to have to sweat so in church on Sunday mornings.

"Should we peek in the windows? Sneak in the back?"

Olivia was running out of patience. Huck understood. "I think we'll start with the for-rent property and peek in windows there. Then when we're around back, I'll cross that little picket fence and have a look through some back windows of our target house. That way if no one's home and the back door is unlocked, I can have a look around without the lady in the rocking chair noticing."

"You mean *we*, right?"

He made a face. "If there's any breaking and entering, you should leave that to me."

She rolled her eyes and climbed out of the vehicle.

Somehow he'd known that wasn't going to work.

He waved at the lady on the porch as they crossed the street. She paused in her fanning but didn't wave back.

Huck snapped a pic of the for-rent sign with its contact info for the rocking lady's benefit. They climbed the steps and peeked in the front door and windows. Then they chatted about the size of the yard and the closeness to the street as they strolled around back. Huck made the first move toward the other property. He stepped across the short picket fence and walked quickly to the back door. Olivia followed close behind him.

Through the window in the door, the kitchen and part of the living room beyond it were visible. No furniture that he could see. He used his shirttail to grasp the knob and give it a turn, and the lock released with little effort. He opened the door.

He hesitated, turned to Olivia. "Don't touch anything. No need to leave incriminating evidence."

She nodded.

The kitchen cabinets were mostly bare. A few canned goods and a box of crackers. The dining room was part of the kitchen, but there was no table. A wide cased opening led into the living room of the small bungalow. The only furniture was a portable chair like the ones people used for camping or ball games. No papers, letters or personal items lying around.

The rest of the house was the same. No furniture. There was a sleeping bag in one of the two bedrooms. Soap in the shower stall. Someone had been staying here under the radar.

Huck checked the sleeping bag. Empty.

A few minutes more of searching and they still found nothing.

"We should go," he said, "before the lady next door gets suspicious."

Olivia exhaled a big breath and nodded her agreement. They followed the same path back to the other house and pretended to discuss the property's options as they made their way back to his SUV. Olivia stared out the window as they drove away.

"I'm beginning to think we're never going to find any answers," she said, her voice distant.

Huck reached for her hand, gave it a squeeze. "We're just cutting through the weeds right now," he assured her. "We'll get to the flowers soon."

His instincts warned they were far closer than either of them understood.

Firefly Lane, 9:00 p.m.

OLIVIA WAS GLAD to be home. She was emotionally exhausted, and she just wanted some quiet time.

No. She *needed* quiet time. No thinking or talking about the possibilities in this case. Just turn it off and relax.

She climbed out of the shower and dried her body, grateful for those long minutes under the hot spray of water and away from the rest of the world.

Once her hair was dry and she'd dressed in one of her grandmother's nightshirts, she opened the door. The scent of bacon frying had her mouth watering. She wandered into the kitchen, where Huck had just set two plates filled with scrambled eggs and bacon on the table.

"It's not exactly a gourmet dinner," he warned, "but it's edible."

"Smells great."

Olivia dug in. She didn't slow down or chat until she was finished. Then she felt stuffed.

"I should not have eaten all that." She put her hand to her stomach. "But it was wonderful."

Huck finished off his. "Good. Hopefully that makes up for my last disappointing attempt at cooking."

She laughed and together they cleaned up the mess he'd made. Strangely, she felt more relaxed than she had in ages. Maybe it was about having hit bottom emotionally. There was nowhere to go but up.

Huck tossed the towel he'd used to dry dishes onto the counter. "It's my turn for that hot shower."

"Go on. I think I might see what's happening in the news. I feel like I've been off the grid for forever."

Sometimes getting away from the news and social media was beneficial. Willy had insisted that social media was just another way to distract ourselves from real life. Olivia was pretty sure he was right.

She turned on the television and scanned the channels for five or ten minutes, but her mind wasn't on the screen or the talking heads whose voices filled the air. She couldn't keep her thoughts from drifting down the hall to the man in that shower. How had she pretended he didn't exist all this time?

He'd done the same to her, she supposed.

Didn't matter. Not anymore. It was time they put that behind them and defined how they would do *this* going forward.

Friends. They could be friends. They had both agreed.

But the feelings churning inside her right now were not exactly the sort she would feel for a friend. The need was overwhelming… fierce. She needed more than just friendship. She needed to feel his arms around her and his mouth on hers.

Olivia closed her eyes and fought the building urgency.

She needed to calm down. To pull back and to…think this through better.

The sound of the door opening and his bare feet in the hall was the last straw. She stood. Threw down the remote and rushed around the sofa and toward him. He stood just outside the bathroom door with only jeans hugging his body.

Her heart beat so hard breathing was impossible. She walked straight up to him. He stared at her now, the towel he'd used slipping to the floor. She put her arms around his neck and tiptoed to reach his mouth with her own.

She kissed him hard with the urgency driving her. He held back, slowed her down, which only made her more frantic.

"Liv," he whispered against her lips, "we need to slow this down."

She plowed her fingers into his damp hair and pulled his mouth back to hers.

A blast drowned out the heavy sound of their breathing and the voices still humming from the television.

Huck drew back, his eyes going from dazed to focused in a single heartbeat. He set her aside, went back into the bathroom and returned with his gun.

"Stay put," he warned, and then he was gone.

The haze of need vanished in that instant, and Olivia whirled around.

He'd already disappeared into the kitchen or to the front door.

She rushed after him.

Another whoosh and then something like an explosion made her jump.

Huck stood staring out the window over the sink, his phone to his ear. Part of her felt frozen in some crazy dream as she heard him give the address and tell whoever he'd called to hurry.

Another sound outside had her moving forward, her gaze zeroing in on that window.

Flames.

Flames flickered high in the darkness.

Something was on fire.

Olivia shook herself and rushed closer.

The shed.

The shed was on fire.

Chapter Eleven

Firefly Lane
Saturday, June 10, 2:00 a.m.

Olivia stood at the back steps and stared at
the dying embers of Willy's beloved shed. All
those beautiful photographs and the film…all
Gran's paintings. Not to mention the equipment and the things the two of them had cher-
ished. Every little thing from the paint brushes
to the camera lenses.

Gone. All gone.

Firefighters had wet down the barn, the nearest trees and shrubbery as well as the cabin in
hopes of preventing sparks from igniting a second fire. Olivia leaned against the wall of the
cabin and watched the final steps of rolling up
hoses and preparing to leave now that the fire
was out. Spotlights showcased their work like
dancers on a stage.

204 *Murder at Sunset Rock*

Huck and Sheriff Decker stood in the middle of the fray.

Olivia had wept like a child, but sometime after midnight resignation had set in and kicked all the other emotions aside. It was done. There was nothing she could do to bring any of it back.

Willy was gone. The biggest part of him that had remained was gone.

This place would never be the same. Never.

She closed her eyes and wished the smell of destruction would diminish. Wished the damned bugs fluttering around the porch light would go away.

"Hey."

Olivia opened her eyes. Huck stared down at her, traces of soot smudged on his face. The worry in his eyes made her wish they could go back inside and lose themselves in more of those kisses they had shared before…this. She glanced at the ongoing efforts of the fire-fighters. They would be leaving soon, and she deeply appreciated all that they had done, but it was a total loss. Not their fault. It just was.

"We found a couple gasoline cans. Decker will take them in for processing."

Beyond Huck, she saw the sheriff walking away from the shed carrying the two red cans.

Plastic ones. Not one of the metal ones Willy had for his lawn mower.

The fire hadn't been an accident.

The resignation collapsed into something more desolate.

"You should go inside," Huck said. "Try to get some sleep. I'll be in when this is finished."

She wanted to say it was already finished, but she couldn't find her voice. Instead, she nodded and did as he suggested.

Rather than collapse on the sofa as was her first thought, she trudged to the bathroom, peeled off her smoky clothes and climbed into the shower to wash away the smoke and soot. Her hands did the work with the soap and shampoo from memory because her brain had officially shut down. She wasn't sure how long she stood beneath the spray of water, but it had turned cold when a knock on the door jarred her from the trance.

"You okay in there, Liv?"

Shivering now, she shut off the water. "Fine. I'll be out in a minute."

She found a towel and dried her skin and hair. The idea of blowing it dry was more than she could manage putting into action. She grabbed the nightshirt hanging on the back of the bathroom door. The soft cotton felt good against her skin. She stared at her reflection and couldn't help playing the words the woman from the corner market had said. *He had a picture of you...'cause you're dangerous.*

Why would that PI, Louis Rogers, have had a picture of Olivia?

And why on earth would he say she was dangerous? She had never met the man. She hadn't been in Hamilton County since Christmas.

It made no sense.

She still had no idea why Willy would have hidden her contact information. If he had hired the PI, why would he give him a photo of Olivia and have him look for her?

She was too tired to think about this anymore. She opened the door and stepped into the hall.

"You okay?"

Huck stood in the hall, hands on his hips. He looked so worried.

"I'm okay. Give the water heater a minute to catch up."

She walked into the main room without a glance beyond the windows. The firefighters and their equipment would be gone by now, but she couldn't bear to see the devastation, even lit by nothing more than the moon.

Her emotions needed a reprieve.

She went to her room, ignored the spray-painted words on the wall, tore away the old poster and then threw back the covers. She climbed into her bed. If sleep would pull her under quickly, she might just survive this night.

Instead, she lay there, eyes wide open. She heard every drop of water fall in the shower. Imagined it sliding over Huck's skin. She squeezed her eyes shut and banished the thought. Eventually the bathroom door opened, and the scent of soap and his skin drifted through the air. Her entire being longed to have him hold her.

She listened to him move through the house, checking doors and windows. When he wandered back into the hall, she held her breath, bit her lips together to prevent calling out to him.

He paused at her door. "Liv, you asleep?"

Don't answer. Don't answer.

"No." *Fool.*

"Everything is locked up. I'll be on the couch if you need me."

She told herself to say goodnight or okay… or to just keep quiet and let him walk away.

Impossible.

"Huck?"

"Yeah?"

She opened her eyes. He stood in the doorway, backlit by the dim light in the hall. Maybe if he'd been wearing a shirt...maybe if she hadn't been so weak...

"I need you here with me."

For a single endless moment he stayed right where he was.

Her heart twisted with disappointment. He was smarter than her.

Then he moved into the room. "You sure about that?"

Heart racing now, she nodded. "Yes."

She drew the covers back as he approached the bed. "I need you, Huck."

Rather than take off his jeans, he climbed into the bed, pulled the covers over himself. "I'll stay right here until you wake up."

She snuggled closer. "Hold me, please."

He tucked one arm around her and pulled her into him. "For as long as you want."

One word echoed through her, but she didn't dare say it out loud. She told herself it was the pain talking. The uncertainty. The loss. Whatever it was, that word just kept echoing.

Always.

8:00 a.m.

RINGING WOKE HER.

Olivia's eyes opened. The sound came again. A cell. Not hers. Wrong ringtone.

She threw back the cover and sat up. Her head ached. Eyes felt raw. Throat too. All the smoke, she decided. She found a pair of jeans and a shirt in her closet. The jeans were ragged, as was the style back in high school. A tee with a Life Is Good logo was the best choice. Her favorite pair of leather sandals caught her attention, and she tugged those on. Still fit. Worn comfortable. A look in the mirror over the dresser had her gasping. Her hair was a wreck. Happened when she went to bed with it wet. A thorough brushing and a ponytail holder took care of that problem. Nothing she could do about the red-rimmed eyes.

The smell of coffee had her making her way to the kitchen. Huck stood at the sink, staring out the window. At the rubble, she surmised. A stab of pain sliced through her. She walked to the counter and poured herself a cup of coffee.

He smiled at her. "Good morning."

How did he look so damned rested…so un-marred by last night's events? Staring at him, dozens of memories from spending all those hours snuggled up with him in bed flashed one after the other in her head. The feel of his bare chest…his muscled arms. A powerful thigh nestled between hers. The smell of his skin.

She blinked. "Morning." A sip of coffee made

her wince. Too hot. She should have paid better attention. "Who called?"

"That was the PI's assistant. She found something she thought might help."

Olivia's mood lifted instantly.

"She spoke with one of the sources we weren't able to reach. He said Rogers had asked a lot of questions about a private mental-health clinic on Pineville Road. Right off Moccasin Bend Road. Since it's unrelated to any of his other cases, she thought it might be part of the Ballard case."

"Isn't Moccasin Bend like a state hospital?" Her mind raced to make some sort of connection to Willy or to herself. Or perhaps to her parents.

"It is, but this isn't that one. It's a private facility that just happens to be in that same area. I helped a deputy escort a patient there once. Rich guy from over in Emerald Valley."

"We should check it out."

"Drink your coffee," he suggested. "I'll have a look around outside, and then I'll be ready."

Olivia turned her back to the counter and the window over the sink. She wasn't sure she could bear to look just yet.

When she'd finished her coffee, she went back to her room and looked for a slightly less casual shirt. She would hate to be denied entrance to the posh clinic because she looked like a vagrant. A pink wrap top. Dressed up the jeans. Good enough.

She grabbed her bag and locked up. Huck waited for her on the porch.

"You ready?" His gaze lingered on the blouse.

She wondered if he remembered it. It was that old. "I'm ready if you are."

Olivia waited until they were headed down the mountain to ask, "Any ideas on how this clinic might be connected to my family?"

"None at all." He slowed for a turn. "While I was having a look around outside, I even called my mom and asked if she recalled anyone Willy or Joyce might have known being committed for any reason. She said not that she remembered. If anything like that happened, it was kept extra quiet."

Which meant it was still possible. "Maybe my mother. But she's been dead for what, twenty-six years? I can't see how that would be relevant."

The PI's words about her being dangerous reverberated again.

"I don't know where this is going," Huck offered, "but it's possible his interest in this clinic had nothing to do with your case. The assistant can't be sure."

"She said that?" Olivia decided Huck might be couching the information in hopes of making her feel better.

"She said it wasn't related to any of his other cases."

Which meant it was related to Willy's case, Olivia mused. "That's what I thought."

"Let's not borrow trouble," Huck countered with a pointed look in her direction.

A new thought sucker-punched her. "Tell me the truth, Huck. Did I ever have any issues that for some reason I'm not remembering?"

He came to a full stop at a red light maybe more abruptly than he'd intended. "You did not."

She breathed a little easier. "Good. Thanks." With all that was going on, she couldn't help but wonder if she was the one with issues.

The drive took half an hour. The wooded area along Moccasin Bend Road was flanked on both sides by the Tennessee River and looked more like a national park. But that wasn't the case at all. At one end of the road was the well-known state hospital, and at the other was where the road became Pineville and split off toward a more industrial area. Just before that split their destination, the Pineville Institute, stood in the woods well off the road. Oddly, along the way there was at least one hiking trail, a golf course and an archaeological district. The city of Chattanooga lay just across the river. None of it really fit together, as if the various parts had been shaken and then tossed out to fall where they might.

Huck eased his SUV into a parking space. A few cars were already in the lot. Olivia hoped since it was Saturday, it was a visitation day, and that would make it easier for them to get inside.

"What's our strategy?" she asked, turning to the man who made her heart skip a beat. Not a good thing, she feared. As much as she wanted to recapture some aspect of their relationship, they were different people now with vastly different lives. Then again, it hadn't felt that way last night when she had lain in his arms feeling safe and warm…and wanting.

"We go in, mingle a bit if possible. Flash around the official pic of Rogers I snatched from the internet. If we're questioned, I flash my badge and ask to see whoever is in charge." While he talked, he tucked his weapon into the glove box and locked it.

"Let's do it then."

They climbed out. He locked the doors as they walked toward the entrance. The clinic looked more like a palatial home. Olivia could only imagine the cost of being a resident in a place like this. Judging by the vehicles in the lot, money wasn't a problem.

Inside was cool. The entrance doors opened to a large, stately lobby that reminded her of one she might find in an elegant New York City hotel. The reception desk looked exactly like a check-in or concierge's counter.

Olivia hung back as Huck approached the counter. He showed his badge. "I'm looking for whoever is in charge."

The younger man behind the counter smiled widely. "Mr. Cyrus is the deputy administrator. Though he isn't usually in on Saturdays, he is in today. He's currently in a meeting. If you don't mind waiting, I'm sure he won't be more than half an hour."

"I'll wait," Huck said.

He joined Olivia at the table in the center of the room. Large bouquets of fresh-cut flowers stood in glass vases atop the table. The smell cloying.

"Half an hour," Huck said. "The manager on duty is named Cyrus."

Didn't sound familiar to Olivia. "What are the odds he'll answer our questions?"

"Not good," Huck admitted, his gaze following the visitors moving on past a set of French doors.

"You thinking the same thing I'm thinking?" she asked, pretending to admire the flowers that basically provided great cover for their position.

"Maybe." His gaze settled on those French doors.

"You hang around out here," she suggested. "Go back to the counter and chat with the man there from time to time. I'll go on in like I'm an authorized visitor. I'll float around and see what I can find."

"I don't know about separating," he argued.

"It's a secure facility," she reminded him. "What could go wrong?"

For two beats, she was sure he would argue. Instead, he exhaled a worried breath. "Just be careful. I'll take a seat closer to the doors, right in front of that desk, where I can be seen."

Olivia nodded. "I'll mingle." When the next cluster of visitors wandered by, she joined the group.

Once she was beyond the French doors, she stayed with the group for a bit longer. Another lobby, not quite so elaborate, was on the right. Most of the group filtered in that direction, leaving Olivia with just one other woman. The woman moved farther down the wide corridor.

The next large space they encountered reminded Olivia of the conservatories she'd seen in Europe. Lots of glass and loads of enormous plants. Numerous conversation areas, some with sofas and chairs, others with larger tables surrounded by chairs. A counter on the far side was stocked with refreshments. Olivia turned away when the attendant monitoring the refreshments glanced her way.

Olivia moved on, pretending to know exactly where she was going. The corridor split into two narrower halls. She went right. Doors lined the hall, each with a number. She wondered if these were the residents' rooms. Being in this area might get her kicked out. She scanned for cameras. Spotted two.

Damn it.

She walked faster, reached an exit door and walked out. A large patio spread out before her. Tables shaded by umbrellas dotted the space, each conversation area adorned with potted plants. Several tables were occupied. Straight ahead was a long, shallow pond that cut through the stone landscape. Koi fish glided leisurely through the crystal clear water.

Olivia turned around and decided her best option was to show the PI's photo to employees. They all wore the same uniform, blue suits, some with trousers, others with skirts.

A woman floated around the tables, smiling, removing empty drink cups and chatting. Olivia sat down at a table in her path. When the woman reached her, she flashed the photo and asked, "Have you seen this man? I was told he'd been bothering guests here."

Olivia held her breath and waited for a response. The lady in blue shook her head. Her gaze narrowed as she leaned closer.

"I haven't seen him. Are you part of the new security?" she asked. "The undercover ones? I heard they had put new people in place after what happened."

Olivia's pulse skittered. "It's state mandated."

The woman glanced around. "It's crazy. In forty-two years, they haven't had an escape until now."

Clocking the movements of the others in the room, Olivia assured her, "We intend to see that it never happens again."

"We'll all feel safer," the other woman said before progressing on to the next table.

Heart pounding with the charge of adrenaline, Olivia stood and walked away. She reentered the clinic through a different door. This one took her back to the large room with the conversation areas and the refreshment counter. She walked straight up to the woman there and asked the same question, showing the photo.

The woman's eyebrows went up. "I can't say

that I've seen him." Her gaze narrowed. "Do you have reason to believe he was involved in the trouble over in D wing?"

Olivia gave a solemn nod. "It's very possible. Have you been in the area today? It's important that we monitor closely with the visitors coming in and out."

Olivia had no clue what she was talking about. She was just going with the flow and hoping like hell she didn't screw up this unexpected cover. Maybe she had missed her calling.

"I was over there a few minutes ago." She hitched her head in the direction Olivia had gone earlier. "All was quiet."

"Good to hear." Olivia glanced at the woman's name tag. "Thank you, Susan."

Olivia wandered on, following that wide corridor once more. This time when she reached the end, she went left. A side staircase waited at the end. Beyond the staircase was another exit. She weighed whether to take the stairs but decided the exit might prove more beneficial since the woman with the refreshments had said "over in D wing" not "up in D Wing." Sounded like a separate area.

Beyond this exit was a sidewalk leading to a maze of buildings. Olivia smiled. Hoped she was fast enough to avoid security noticing someone not wearing a blue suit in this area.

She passed buildings B and C and strolled straight toward D, which sat the farthest from the main building. At the entrance, the door was secured with an access panel that required a badge or other card to swipe. Unlike the other buildings, this one had no windows. She decided to walk around the building to look for other entrances. Maybe someone had propped open a side door or was standing outside to have a smoke. Though she doubted smoking was allowed anywhere on the campus.

Olivia had no idea how much longer her ruse would work. She listened for the sound of footfalls above the rush of blood in her ears. Her nerves jangled with equal parts excitement and worry. She could imagine security rushing to drag her away.

She spotted a patio at the back of the building, but this one was very different from the last. This one was austere with concrete tables and benches and a high fence around the space. No plants or umbrellas at this one. No getting beyond the fence either.

A lone woman sat at a table on the far side of the patio. Olivia walked in that direction, staying close to the fence. The woman's head came up when she noticed Olivia. As Olivia moved closer to her side of the concrete expanse, the woman grew visibly agitated. Her body tensed, her face seemed to pale. She looked older than Olivia but it was difficult to say precisely how much.

When Olivia had gotten as close as she could with the fence in her way, the woman stood, her movements stilted. She walked toward the fence, toward Olivia, her eyes growing ever wider.

"What're you doing here?" The words were hissed almost under her breath. She looked around as if she expected someone to see them.

Uncertain whether to ask questions or just play along, Olivia smiled. "Hello."

The woman's head moved side to side so hard Olivia couldn't see how she didn't get whiplash. "You said you were never coming back. Ever."

Heart thumping frantically, Olivia opted to play along. "I had to."

The woman took a step away. "You shouldn't have come back. Now they'll know."

She ran away. Snatched at the handle of the door leading into the windowless building.

Olivia couldn't move. She stood there…frozen. How could that woman possibly know her?

Firefly Lane, 12:00 p.m.

LUCKILY, BY THE time the deputy administrator, Cyrus, had warned Huck he would need a warrant to be inside the facility, Olivia had returned to the lobby. Huck had known something was very, very wrong when he saw her face.

As they had driven away from the clinic, Huck had been seriously worried about Olivia. She hadn't said a word since exiting that clinic. Not until they were across the river and headed up the mountain did she break her silence and tell him what happened. He'd struggled for something to say that would possibly explain what the woman had said to Olivia.

But there was only one explanation, and he couldn't go there…not yet.

As he parked behind her SUV at the cabin, he noted that Decker was already there waiting for them. Calling the sheriff and telling him they needed a meeting ASAP had been the only option. Something was way out of bounds here, and to tell the truth, he wasn't sure he could trust his judgment in the matter.

Decker met them on the porch. "What's going on, Monroe? I just got a call from the deputy administrator at Pineville, who says you were up there harassing residents."

"Not true, Sheriff," Huck argued. He wasn't

actually surprised Decker had gotten a call already.

Olivia unlocked and opened the door. "I'm the only one who spoke to a resident," she said before going inside.

Huck waited for the sheriff to go next, then he followed.

Olivia immediately launched into the story about what they had learned from the private investigator's assistant. She didn't slow down long enough for Huck to get a word in edgewise until she was done and had confessed to getting the call, coming up with the idea to go to the clinic and going inside. She summed up her monologue by saying that Huck had only gone along to protect her from herself.

When Decker's attention swung to him, Huck shook his head. "This is not her fault. I—"

"Save it," Decker said. "We all need a good stiff drink, and then we need to talk."

To say his response surprised Huck would be a vast understatement.

Olivia gestured to the sofa. "I'll get Willy's bourbon."

Huck rounded up three glasses and joined his boss. He chose the chair opposite the sofa. Having the coffee table between them felt like the right move.

Decker said nothing until Olivia sat down on the sofa and poured the bourbon. They each tossed back the shot, even Olivia. Huck was impressed that she only winced.

Decker set his glass on the table. "I'm going to tell you what Willy should have told you a long time ago, Olivia."

Huck braced himself. Wished he was closer to her. She looked tired and exhausted and about fifteen years old again. Holding her in his arms last night had broken him over and over. Each time he'd managed to pull himself together, she moved or breathed a little more deeply, and he'd come undone again.

Olivia squared her shoulders. "I'm listening."

"Your mother, Laura, was always a little wild." He shrugged. "Looking back, we should have seen it for what it was." He shook his head. "But we didn't."

When she would have spoken, he held up a hand to stop her. "When she ran off and got involved with your father, Willy and Joyce tried to make the best of it. If she was happy that was all that mattered. But after you were born things went downhill fast."

"What does that mean?" Olivia demanded, her eyes shining with the emotion she could no longer contain.

Huck's gut clenched. He waffled between wanting to hug her and to punch Decker. He hoped to hell all this was necessary. Otherwise he might just lose his job for kicking the guy's butt for putting her through this.

"Laura was mentally unstable, Olivia," he said flatly. "We all pretended it away, but after you were born the clues were undeniable. It wasn't so easy since she and that jerk disappeared frequently. But when they'd come back, it would take her weeks to be right again."

"Depression? Schizophrenia? What are we talking about here?" Olivia demanded.

"The one diagnosis was schizophrenia." He exhaled a big breath. "But who knows. When you were three, he left without her for a while. She basically came undone. She had to be hospitalized. We took her to Pineville. It's private, so we could keep it quiet. Willy didn't want that kind of thing on her record."

"How long was she there?" Huck asked since Olivia seemed to have lost her voice.

"Three months. When she came home, he showed up again, and for a while she seemed to be happy," Decker went on. He stared at the floor a moment. "But then she did something we couldn't pretend away. That loser told her he was planning to leave again, and she lost it. Killed him. I was there. I tried to stop her."

The shock on Olivia's face forced Huck to his feet. He moved to stand next to her. "What the hell?" he demanded of his boss.

"Willy begged me to help him cover it up." Decker shook his head. "I shouldn't have done it, but Joyce was devastated. Willy was falling apart. The bastard was a drifter, had no family. No one was going to miss him. There was Olivia's future to think about. How could we let her grow up with that hanging over her head?"

Huck swore. "You helped Willy cover up a murder?"

Decker nodded. "Having Laura charged with murder wasn't going to bring him back. Wasn't going to help anyone."

Huck rested his hand on Olivia's shoulder, wished he could take her out of here, away from this horror story. "I feel compelled to tell you, sir, that you may want to stop talking at this point."

"No." Olivia looked up at him, the hollow, pained look on her face ripping his heart out. She turned back to Decker. "What happened next?"

Decker took a moment, likely to consider the ramifications of what he was doing. "We buried him and pretended nothing had happened. Laura lapsed into depression. No matter how Willy and Joyce tried, she just wouldn't snap out of it. They took her back to Pineville for a few weeks, and that seemed to help, but then…" He cleared his throat. "She went to the dam and jumped. She'd left a note at home, but by the time Willy got there, it was too late."

Olivia inhaled a sharp breath. She stood. "Thank you for finally telling me the truth."

She pushed past Huck and disappeared out the back door. He stood there, in a kind of shock. Torn between punching his boss and going after her.

"You do what you will with what I've said," Decker announced, pushing to his feet. "She needed the truth. As awful as it is. For the record, I did what I thought was best, and I'd do it again."

He left.

Huck wasn't sure there was any way on earth to fix this, but he had to try.

Chapter Twelve

Huck walked out the back door. Olivia stood on the stone path amid the hundreds of blooming plants bordering each side. If Willy were here, he would say what a perfect shot the scene would make. Her dark ponytail hanging against the pink shirt. The contrast of the silky pink against the worn blue cotton of her jeans. The multitude of colors in the blooms surrounding her and all of it facing a backdrop of blackened rubble where the shed once stood. Beauty and tragedy.

Pulling in a deep breath, Huck moved in behind her. He bowed his head, could smell the sweet scent of shampoo in her hair.

She whirled around, faced him. "Did you know any of this?"

The misery on her face made him want to pull her into his arms and promise her anything. She was too hurt and angry to allow him to touch her right now. He shook his head in answer to her question. "I can't imagine how hard it must have been for Willy to carry that burden all this time."

"He lied to me." Tears welled in her eyes. "I can see how he rationalized this scheme in the beginning. But not now, after all these years." Her breath caught. "There's no excuse."

"You're angry," Huck said. "When you've had some time to think, you might be able to see his reasoning."

She shook her head. "I don't see that happening." She laughed then, the sound painful. "It's such a cliché. Everything I've believed my entire life is a lie."

Huck took her by the shoulders and gave her a gentle shake. "No. Willy and Joyce loved you. More than anything. Laura loved you, the best she could. I might not remember her, but you're her daughter. I can't imagine she was that different from you when you get down to the basics. Whatever illness plagued her, I'm betting she did the best she could. Everything your family did was to protect you."

She stared up at him, the tears sliding down her cheeks gutting him. "It's still all lies any way you look at it."

He had to find a way to make her see…

"I lied to you."

She stared at him. New pain settling into her features.

"When I left, it wasn't because I didn't want to be with you anymore. It was because I didn't want to hold you back."

She shook free of his touch. "What the hell are you talking about?"

"I couldn't take being apart so much. So one Saturday morning, I drove over to surprise you." He swallowed back the doubt. "I watched you and your friends all weekend. Watched the way this one guy watched you…laughed with you. I was just a rookie cop. No way I'd ever be able to offer you the kind of future that whole college scene, guys like that one, could offer you."

She held her hands up as if she felt the need to protect herself. "You didn't say a word. Why didn't you talk to me?"

"I couldn't. I just needed to let it go."

"You mean, let me go." Anger lashed across her face. "You threw us away because you…"

"I thought I was doing the right thing." Damn. This was not helping at all.

"You took the coward's way out. It was easier than fighting for me—not that a fight would have been required." She clenched her fists at her sides as if she needed to hold herself back from punching him. "You gave up and walked away when there was no reason to. That guy—the big flirt everyone in our group complained about—was just a jerk trying to get in every freshman's pants. He was no one to me. And you—" The breath shuddered out of her. "You were everything."

Before he could find the words to say, she shouldered past him and went back into the house. Well, hell. He'd screwed that one up big time. So much for his big confession. Idiot!

OLIVIA SLAMMED THE back door shut and stormed through the house and into her room. This was too much. She could not think about all the lies anymore. The most urgent issue at the moment, in her opinion—not that she was a cop—was who the hell was behind Willy's death? Who killed the private investigator? And who burned down the damned shed?

She grabbed a tee and changed from the pink blouse, which was the best one she had available here.

Dragging her fingers through her ponytail to free it, she had to ask why the hell she was still here.

Willy was dead. The shed was destroyed. She could just change the locks on the cabin and walk away.

Staying wouldn't change one damned thing.

Fury roared through her. Except she wasn't going anywhere until she found the person who hurt Willy. He'd protected Olivia her entire life—even if some of his decisions weren't the best ones. She loved him. She owed him. Nothing was going to stop her from getting this done.

She dug through her closet and found her sneakers.

"I made the wrong choice."

She turned from the closet to find Huck standing in her doorway, looking for all the world like a lost puppy with nowhere to go.

"You did." She steadied herself, tamped back the rising anger. She walked to her dresser and dug out a pair of socks, then sat down on the bed. She took her time, putting on the socks and then slipping on the sneakers. "You should have trusted me. Talked to me. Instead, you threw me away."

He closed his eyes, shook his head. "Don't say that." His eyes opened once more, and he searched hers. "I would never do that. I thought—at the time—I was doing the right thing. It was a while before I realized I was wrong."

She stalked over to where he stood still bracketed by that doorway as if it might somehow protect him from the coming storm. Not happening. "And just when did you have this epiphany? Was it after the fifth time I tried to call you? Or after I came back home and knocked on your door until my knuckles bled? Or maybe it was months after I had cried my-self to sleep every damned night."

If she'd sucker-punched him, he wouldn't have looked any more damaged.

She wanted to be glad, but somehow couldn't muster the triumphant feeling.

"I was wrong, Liv. I would've done anything to make it up to you, but I realized it was too late by then."

"Coward." She pressed a hand to his chest and pushed him back from the door.

She had stuff to do.

He followed her out of the house. Let him. He wasn't going to stop her.

In the barn, she searched until she found a shovel. Then she rummaged around for a sec-ond one. When she found it behind the rakes and hoes, she grabbed it and tossed it toward him. To her surprise, he caught it.

"If you're going to keep hanging around," she said, her voice a little wobbly despite the anger, "you can help me."

"Okay."

He might feel differently if he bothered to

ask what she planned to do. Since he didn't, she headed away from the barn and the house and that damned pile of charred metal that was once the shed. She didn't stop until she reached that big old oak so close to the cliffs it was a miracle its roots went deep enough to hold it in place.

She stopped next to her mother's grave. "Both my parents are dead. Willy's gone. Gran. Then who's doing this? Who would have a motive to want to hurt me or hurt the people I love? Think about it. Why wouldn't Gran or Willy want to be buried here, next to their only child—their daughter? That alone should have set off warning bells ages ago. Something isn't right about this grave."

A realization dawned and his head moved side to side. "Liv, I get what you're saying. But you can't do this."

"I can." She swallowed back the tears that crowded into her throat. "You can either help me or you can walk away. You've done it before."

He stared at the ground a moment, properly chastised. "What do you expect to find?"

She lifted her shoulders in an exaggerated shrug. "I don't know. Maybe some proof of what the truth really is."

"Decker said she's dead." Huck glanced toward the grave at Olivia's feet.

"Then why was Rogers looking for her? Why did that patient at Pineville asked me why I was back?"

"I don't know what the PI was doing, but Decker said your mother was a patient at Pineville."

"He did," she agreed. "But the woman who spoke to me was thirty-five at most. Are you telling me she remembers my mother from more than twenty-five years ago?"

Huck held her gaze for a moment. "You didn't mention that she was so young."

"It wasn't relevant until Decker's confession." The way Huck was looking at her now had anticipation zinging through her. He was thinking the same thing. If it wasn't Olivia the woman had seen...then who?

"You'll need gloves."

"We both will," she admitted.

They walked back to the barn together. No one spoke. Finding the gloves was easy because Gran had been meticulous at organization and Willy had ensured it all stayed that way.

Huck's hands barely fit into a pair of Willy's leather work gloves. Gran's gloves fit Olivia perfectly.

The walk back to that big old oak was equally quiet. They'd both said more than enough. There was nothing left to do but dig.

By the time they were standing in a hole the length of a coffin and about waist deep, Huck paused. "We should take a break. Drink some water."

He'd long ago discarded his shirt. The tee beneath was streaked with sweat and dirt.

Olivia's tee was damp. Her arms ached. She was thirsty, but she wasn't stopping. "Not yet."

She dug her shovel into the dirt. Hit something. Probably another rock. "Damned rocks," she muttered.

Apparently convinced she wasn't stopping, Huck began digging again.

She crouched down and dragged her finger around the rock. She'd discovered that to get them out, she had to dig around the damned things until they were loosened from the soil. She alternated between prying around it with her shovel and scrapping away what she could with her gloved fingers.

White peeked from the dirt.

The color wasn't the same as the other rocks she'd unearthed. She swiped at the dirt, pushing aside a little more.

A hole in the rock appeared…then another. Not holes. Eye sockets.

Olivia tumbled back. Let go of her shovel. The handle banked off Huck's broad shoulder.

He stared at what she'd revealed. He muttered something unintelligible as he dropped to his knees. He tore off the gloves and scratched at the dirt around the skull. Moving by rote, she joined him, scratching and tugging.

Once the skull was free, Huck sat it on the ground next to the base of the tree, away from the pile of dirt on the other side of the hole they'd dug.

More bones...fragments of fabric. The better part of a sneaker.

Olivia sat back, the sneaker's rubber sole held between her gloved fingers. Not a woman's sneaker. Too long...too wide. This was a man's sneaker.

Her gaze collided with Huck's.

He started digging again, his movements as frantic as the pounding in her chest.

The other sneaker or what was left of it appeared. Then the parts of a belt buckle. Rivets from a pair of name-brand jeans...nothing was left of the cotton.

Olivia's fingers closed around an object... black...wallet.

She pulled it from the dirt. Stared at it a moment then handed it to Huck. She couldn't open it...no way.

He opened the wallet; deteriorating pieces fell away. His dirt-crusted fingers struggled, tugging at what Olivia hoped was an ID of some sort.

When it was free from the plastic slip, he held it out for her inspection.

Driver's license. *Kasey Aldean*.

Olivia stared at the bones spread over the grass then at the image of a young man on the driver's license.

This was her father's grave.

Her father's remains.

Then where the hell was her mother?

Chapter Thirteen

6:00 p.m.

"We wanted to save you the additional pain," Sheriff Decker explained.

Olivia wanted to scream! Instead she steeled herself against the raging emotions. "What're you saying?"

Decker stared at the bones scattered on the ground. "I told you Willy and I hid his body to protect your mother. This is where we buried him."

Huck stood next to her, but so far he had allowed her to do the talking. She appreciated his deference to her need to demand answers.

"Where is my mother buried?"

"She isn't." Decker's shoulders sagged. "You know how the waters are around that dam. We searched for days to no avail. Her body was never recovered. I guess you can say she's buried in the river." His shoulders squared then as if he'd decided there would be no more appeasement from him. He gave Olivia a firm look. "You need to stop this, Liv. You need to get on with your life. Digging around in that part of the past will never bring you the peace you're looking for. What's done is done, and some things are best left alone."

With that, he gave Huck a nod and he walked away. Huck followed him. Probably had a few things of his own to say. This news about the cover-up had shaken him too. To find the remains had been the last straw.

Olivia couldn't remember when she had felt so angry…so damned disappointed. She blinked. Realized it had been ten years ago when Huck threw away her hopes and dreams. But that had been different. This was… Olivia shook herself, couldn't quite label what the hell this was.

The sheriff. A lawman vested with the power of enforcing the law…wanted her to pretend she hadn't just dug up the remains of a murdered man.

Her father.

His skull hadn't been bashed in. She hadn't seen any sort of damage to any of the other bones. Huck hadn't noticed any readily visible damage either.

Had her mother poisoned him? Shot him?

Olivia squeezed her eyes shut. Didn't matter. She had killed him, and then she'd taken her own life. Had she not once considered how her actions would affect her baby? Or maybe she had known that Olivia would be better off with her grandparents.

She couldn't be here any longer. Olivia walked away from the shallow grave with its bones laid bare on the open ground. She needed to think. To consider all this painful information.

She'd almost reached the house when Huck met her in the middle of the backyard.

"He's gone."

Olivia considered this man—the one person she felt she could still trust. "Do you believe him?"

"Which part?"

"Any part?" Olivia surveyed the yard with all its blooms that had given her grandparents so much pleasure. "Obviously, my father is dead. I'm sure Willy wouldn't have helped cover up his murder without a very compelling reason, so I suppose it's true that my mother killed him."

Huck pulled out his cell and tapped a few keys. Olivia waited to hear whatever he had to say.

"I can find your mom's obit on here, but nothing about her death or a drowning at the dam."

Olivia shook her head. "That makes no sense. Wouldn't that have been on the news?"

Huck nodded. "Definitely. Unless they covered it up too."

"They certainly never told me she took her own life."

"Decker wasn't the sheriff then, but he was an up-and-coming chief deputy," Huck pointed out. "He could have called in a favor with a private search and rescue team."

Olivia lifted her chin and offered a scenario of her own. "What if she never jumped? What if she just left that note and ran away?"

Huck nodded slowly. "Then suddenly came back recently for reasons that worried Willy. He hires a PI to try and figure out what her game is and…well, you know how that ended."

"I have to know for sure." Olivia moistened her lips, struggled with the conflicting emotions. "If she's alive, I want to find her. If she hurt Willy, I want…"

Huck reached out, took her hand and gave it a reassuring squeeze. "We can figure that part out as soon as we determine where she is."

Olivia nodded. He was right. "We should go back to that house, where the sleeping bag was. Maybe she was staying there, and the guy watching for her just never saw her."

"We'll start there."

Vine Street, 7:10 p.m.

THE STREET WAS QUIET. At this hour on Saturday evening, most people were probably out for the evening or inside having dinner and watching their favorite television program. They would have gotten here twenty or so minutes ago, but they'd had to clean themselves up after digging up those bones. Olivia hadn't wanted to take the time for showers, so they'd washed up, changed clothes in record time and headed out.

Huck parked at the curb in front of the house that was for rent, the one they'd used as a decoy to see the one next to it. And like before, the old lady sat on her porch rocking the evening away.

"I'm going to talk to her," Olivia said.

"We've got nothing to lose," Huck agreed. They had already been in the house and found nothing useful other than evidence that someone had been staying there.

They climbed out and headed to the lady's front porch. She stopped rocking and watched their approach.

Olivia opened the gate to her picket fence. "Good evening," she said. "Do you have a moment for a few questions about the house for rent?"

Olivia stopped at the bottom of the steps. Huck stood behind her.

The older lady surveyed them a long moment, lifted her chin as if she might banish them from her property. "I thought you were looking at the one for sale."

Huck almost grinned. She remembered them.

"Yes, ma'am," Olivia said. "We had a look at it too, but it's the rental that we're really interested in."

She grunted as if uncertain if she believed Olivia. "Well, come on up here on the porch so I can hear you better."

Huck thought she was hearing just fine, but he was grateful for the invitation.

Olivia climbed the steps and waited for Huck to join her.

"Take a load off," the lady offered.

Olivia took the matching rocker next to her; Huck settled on the swing.

"Thank you." Olivia smiled. "I'm Olivia Ballard, and this is my friend Deputy Detective Huck Monroe."

The woman eyed him suspiciously before turning back to Olivia. "I saw you before."

Huck noticed that she didn't give her name. He didn't blame her. They were strangers.

"Yes, ma'am," Olivia agreed. "When we looked at the house next door."

The woman shook her head. "Maybe your friend don't know it, but I saw you going in and outta that house like you owned the place."

Olivia frowned. "You're mistaken. It wasn't me."

The woman laughed. "You might have your deputy friend here fooled, but I watched you coming and going ever since Monday night. It wasn't even dark when I saw you creeping around."

IT TOOK EVERY ounce of willpower Huck possessed not to speak up, but he clamped his jaws shut and let Olivia run with this. Her eyes widened, and she nodded.

"Sorry, I didn't mean to bother you. I wasn't sure you saw me, but now I know. It's important that no one finds out I was here."

The lady shook her head. "No bother. I figured you was hiding from somebody. I wasn't gonna call the police unless you started some trouble. Thelma—" she hitched her head toward the houses farther down the street "—said she talked to you. Said you were real nice." She glanced at Huck. "I guess you found someone to help you figure out whatever trouble you're in."

Olivia nodded. "I did. I'll just check in with Thelma and let her know. Is she home?"

"If that little old red car of hers is in the driveway, she's home." She nodded toward his SUV. "You should've seen it when you parked."

"Thank you." Olivia stood. "It was kind of you not to tell anyone about me."

"You were smart to stay gone when that fella was out there watching. He stayed day and night for two whole days."

"Yes, ma'am."

As they descended the steps, Olivia glanced up at Huck. Her eyes full of uncertainty. He got it. The woman obviously hadn't seen Olivia. She'd seen someone who looked like her. And from her porch, she likely hadn't noticed that the woman she saw was older.

Whatever Decker thought, Huck was pretty damned certain that Laura Ballard was still alive.

Just past the rental house and the one for sale was a small bungalow with a little red car parked in the driveway.

Olivia took a big breath and started up the sidewalk to the small porch. Huck followed.

Before they reached the porch, the occupant of the house—presumably Thelma—opened the wood door. "Are you okay?" she asked through the screen door.

"Thelma?"

The woman blinked, stepped out onto the

porch. "Oh… I thought you were someone else."

"My name is Olivia Ballard," she said. "I need to ask you some questions about the woman who was staying next door."

Thelma nodded. "It's weird how much the two of you look alike." She glanced beyond Olivia to Huck. "He your husband?"

"No. He's my friend."

Huck liked that she called him her friend but…part of him wished she had said he was her husband.

"What questions?" She eyed Olivia with mounting suspicion. "They sent someone looking for her, just like she said they would. I ain't planning to help her be found if she doesn't want to be found."

Huck decided it was time he spoke up. "Ma'am, the woman you met is Laura Ballard, Olivia's mother. What she may not have told you is that she is in danger. The people looking for her may not be as worried about her well-being as Olivia and I are. If you can help us, you'll be helping Laura."

She eyed Huck with more of that suspicion. "I see from that vehicle you're driving, you're a cop. Maybe she don't want no cop to find her either."

"If someone else finds her first," Olivia added, "we may not be able to help her."

Thelma exhaled a big breath. "She escaped that place where she'd been a prisoner for most of her adult life. She said she couldn't trust anyone and that she was worried about her daughter." Her gaze narrowed again. "So that's you?"

Olivia nodded. "I've spent my whole life believing she was dead."

The woman made a face. "I ain't gonna ask how that happened, but she did say the last person she trusted got killed."

Olivia shared a look with Huck. "Did she say who that person was?"

Thelma shook her head. "I don't know. She hasn't been back since that guy was watching the house."

"Did she tell you anything else?" Olivia pressed. "Who kept her prisoner? Why she was never able to escape before?"

"She didn't tell me much, but she did say she'd been trying to get away for years, but all her attempts failed."

Huck passed her a card. "Please call if you hear anything else from her. We want to help, but we can't if we don't find her."

Thelma stared at the card then looked to

Olivia. "You really should help her. They did stuff to her at that place."

Huck felt Olivia stiffen next to him.

"What sort of things?" Olivia asked, her voice thin.

"She didn't go into much, but she did mention shock treatments. She said that was one of the ways they punished her."

Olivia nodded. "Did she seem okay to you?"

Thelma looked put out by the question. "Are you asking me if she seemed crazy?"

"No," Olivia countered, "I'm asking you if she seemed calm or frenzied? Afraid or overly upset?"

"She seemed fine. Determined to find someone to believe her. But she did not seem the least bit agitated or off her meds, so to speak. She acted as normal as you or me."

Olivia nodded. "We'll do all within our power to help her."

The woman watched until they had loaded up and driven away. Olivia sat in silence as Huck navigated the streets.

"I need you to be careful, Liv," he warned, glancing at her as he drove. "We don't know the whole story. Willy would never have gone along with any part of this unless he felt there was no other choice."

Olivia turned to Huck. "I don't know what to trust anymore."

He took her hand in his. "We'll figure it out."

The question that kept ringing in his head was why the hell hadn't Decker told him Olivia's mother was still alive?

Unless he really didn't know.

Firefly Lane, 8:30 p.m.

OLIVIA STILL FELT numb as she unlocked the door and went into the house. She didn't know what to think or to believe.

She wanted to feel hurt that Willy hadn't told her whatever part of all this he knew. If, as Decker said, he'd been protecting his daughter, she could understand. But why not come clean in the past few years? Olivia was a grown woman. She had a right to know the truth.

At the window over the sink, she stared at the rubble that had been his and Gran's prized workplace. How had it all come to this?

She thought about Willy's final days on this earth. He'd had lunch with Madeline. Had he known then that something was wrong? Had Laura already escaped the facility? Was Laura the reason he'd been at the market buying bread and wine? Madeline said she hadn't seen him since lunch on Sunday…so who was he preparing to have dinner with?

At this point, the only reasonable answer was: Laura.

Was Willy who Laura had meant when she said the one person she could trust was dead?

Olivia wished she had been able to ask the woman at Pineville when Laura had escaped, but she'd run away too quickly. She went to the stored photo albums and grabbed the ones with photos of her mother. She collapsed on the sofa and started flipping through the pages, scanning each photo.

Huck sat down next to her. "What're we looking for?"

"This." Olivia tapped a photo of her mother on the beach, a glass in one hand, a bottle of wine dangling from the fingers of the other. "She was a wine drinker." She met Huck's gaze. "What if she was coming here to have dinner with Willy on Sunday night? Maybe the wine and bread were for her."

"We need to find that wine bottle." Huck shot to his feet.

Olivia put the photo album aside and stood. "Willy recycled glass."

They hurried out the mudroom door. Next to the small back porch was the large wheeled garbage can as well as several smaller lidded bins where recyclables were stored.

Olivia opened the bin for glass and picked through the few items. "Nothing here."

Huck opened the larger garbage can.

"Willy wouldn't have tossed it in the trash," Olivia said.

No sooner than the words were out of her mouth, Huck withdrew a wine bottle. His eyebrows rose higher on his forehead. "Maybe Laura tossed it in here. She may have cleaned up after their dinner."

"Maybe." Olivia joined Huck at the garbage can and surveyed the contents. The trash was picked up on Fridays, so whatever was inside would only have been from the weekend leading up to Willy's death. She hadn't tossed anything in there since her arrival. The smell of rotting spaghetti sauce made her wince. The better part of the stick of French bread lay among the noodles and red sauce. "Doesn't look like they ate much."

"Good thing the bottle was on top," Huck said.

He held it gingerly. His fingers touching only the rim of the very top.

"If you'll grab me the largest plastic bag you can find, I'll put the bottle inside and have someone come pick it up and check for prints."

"Good idea."

Olivia hurried into the house, searched the cabinets until she found the plastic storage bags. "Will a gallon size do?"

"Think so."

She grabbed a bag and held it open while Huck eased the bottle inside.

"I'll make the call. Maybe Snelling will pick it up today and put a rush on the processing."

Olivia nodded. "Thanks." She hitched a thumb toward the hall. "I'm going to shower." Truth was she felt totally exhausted. She couldn't risk falling asleep with the odor of dirt clinging to her skin.

Huck was already making the call.

Olivia rounded up a clean nightshirt and locked herself away in the bathroom. She peeled off her clothes and tossed them into the pile with the others they had abandoned today. She turned on and adjusted the water in the shower and stepped into the tub.

She washed her hair, massaged her scalp. The hot water felt good against her sore and tense muscles. Moving the soap over her skin, she felt herself slowly relaxing as she washed the horror of their discovery off her body. Had Willy and Gran known her father was buried there?

The idea that Willy hadn't told her stabbed

deep. She tried to find some logic to rationalize his decision, but nothing felt big enough or strong enough to leave her in the dark this way. Why would he deny her that truth? If Laura truly had some sort of mental illness, Olivia needed to know. So many were hereditary.

The woman's—Thelma's—story about Laura being held prisoner nudged her. Of course, she would feel like a prisoner in a place like Pineville. Some patients who suffered with mental illness were unaware of the trouble. But Thelma had insisted Laura seemed fine. Normal. But even patients with extreme disorders had times of calm clarity.

Olivia couldn't think about this anymore. She shut off the water and got out, dried herself and tugged on the nightshirt. It took some time to brush out her hair, but when it was done she finally felt hungry. By the time she'd blown her hair dry she was starving.

Huck was already scouring the cabinets when she walked into the kitchen. "Looks like we may have to see if we can get something delivered."

"Any of those services available this far out?" Her stomach reminded her she needed to get something ordered now.

Huck pulled out his cell and tapped an app. "Pizza? Mexican or Chinese?"

"Pizza."

A few more taps. "It'll be on our doorstep in thirty-five minutes."

"Great."

"Meanwhile." He walked to the fridge and reached inside. "We can share a beer."

He withdrew the single can. Willy's favorite.

"We can do that."

Huck passed the can to her. "You go ahead. I'm taking my turn in the shower."

"I'll save it for you," she offered.

"Go ahead. I'll figure out something after I shower."

"Wait, is your CSI friend coming?"

Huck paused at the door to the hall. "He came. Picked up the bottle and had some interesting news."

Olivia popped the top on the can. Beer wasn't her favorite recreational drink, but right now she was fairly desperate. "Oh yeah?"

Huck nodded. "According to his wife, who's the chief deputy, Sheriff Decker has resigned, citing personal reasons."

Olivia's jaw dropped. "Are you serious?"

"Chief Deputy Snelling will be acting sheriff for now."

"Do you think all this prompted that decision?" Olivia could certainly see how he would feel compelled to do so considering that his dark secret was out now—at least with her and Huck.

"When he left, I'm fairly certain he understood how we felt about what he'd done."

"He made a bad choice." Olivia had known the man her whole life, but right was right, and he'd been wrong all those years ago. He should have talked Willy into doing the right thing, not jumped in to help him do the wrong thing.

"He did." Huck gave her a nod then disappeared into the hall.

Olivia had never been more thankful for his presence. She sighed. Feeling a sense of relief that surprised her. Her life was upside down right now, but at least she wasn't alone. As she sipped the beer, she wandered through the living area. Studied the painting over the fireplace. Moved on to the other photographs framed and hanging on the walls. She felt such deep regret that the shed had been destroyed. So much history gone.

Had Laura done that?

Was she trying to hide something or trying to tell Olivia something?

If she was out there somewhere and knew Olivia was here, why not come to the door? Talk to her? Olivia certainly hadn't been involved in whatever happened to her. She had no reason not to talk to her and to hear her out.

And what if she is responsible for Willy's death?

Olivia pushed away the voice and that too painful question.

She walked to the door, opened it and stepped out onto the porch. Was her mother here somewhere watching? Waiting for an opportunity to talk to Olivia alone?

Or waiting for an opportunity to kill her?

Olivia finished off the beer and set the empty can on the railing. She moved down the steps and surveyed the yard. Her and Huck's vehicles stood one behind the other. Willy's Defender was parked next to the house. Gran's pots of flowers and mounds of blooming shrubs scented the air, effectively masking the lingering smell of smoke. It was cooler now that the sun had fallen behind the trees, leaving the twilight.

Olivia thought of the bones near the cliff. She should probably feel guilty about leaving them lying there. At some point they would have to call in the find, and the bones would be taken for examination. She wondered if at this point cause of death could be determined.

It happened on the television shows. She supposed it could in real life as well.

She suddenly wondered if she could ever live here again. This had been home to her.

Even though she'd been gone a decade, it had always been home. But the people who had made it home were all gone.

Except Huck. He was back.

A shiver swept over her, and she scolded herself for allowing the sensation. They had been over for a very long time. In spite of what he'd told her, there were some bridges that couldn't be crossed again even if they hadn't been burned completely. But they could be friends. She wasn't losing that.

He was a good man. She couldn't deny how well he'd turned out. She'd heard about his awards and commitment to the community over and over from Willy even when she had not wanted to.

He was even better looking now than he had been as a kid. Very, very good looking if she was honest with herself.

He'd treated her with such respect...more than she had afforded him. She'd wanted him so badly last night. She would have made love with him in a heartbeat...but he'd suggested they slow things down.

She stilled. Then again, maybe there was someone else. Willy had said Huck didn't do relationships, but maybe Willy hadn't known.

She would be a fool to think he didn't have plenty of women interested.

A lump rose into her throat. She reminded herself that she was no longer interested. That she had moved on.

Except none of that was entirely true.

She dated. Had the occasional weeks-or months-long relationship…but never anything serious.

Never anything even remotely close to what she had with him.

Had their mistakes ruined the possibility of their best chance at something real…something permanent?

Whatever else they did or didn't have, he was the one person she could still count on… could still trust.

Was she going to finish this, walk away and pretend that she didn't still care about him… didn't still want him?

If she did…she would never know.

Know what? She swore at herself. Her heart pounding. Every part of her needing…*something*.

No. She did an about-face and headed back into the house. She would not—could not—walk away without knowing. Without being sure.

She locked the door and took a deep breath.

The scent of steamy air drifted to her from the hall, and she followed it there. Huck walked out of the bathroom, the towel he'd used wrapped around his waist.

He smiled. "Sorry. Forgot to grab clean clothes."

She walked straight up to him. "Look me in the eyes," she ordered, "and tell me you don't want me."

He frowned. "What?"

"Tell me you don't want me." She drew in a breath, every nerve in her body sizzling. "I want you to say it, and I'll go into my room, and I won't bother you again."

The expression that slipped over his face—a tenderness that stole her breath. "Why would you think I don't want you?"

"Then show me."

His hands came up to her face, cupped her cheeks. He stared at her lips as his descended there, and then there was nothing else. Only the taste of him…the smell of him and the feel of his body so close to hers.

He kissed her until she melted against him. Her fingers found their way to the towel and pulled it loose from his hips. He lifted her against him. Her legs circled his waist, and he carried her to her room.

Her nightshirt hit the floor, and her panties slid down her legs. He lowered her to the bed and pressed against her. Then there was no thought…there were only sensations. The feel of him inside her. His lips on her breasts. His hands on her skin.

She touched all of him, tracing, remembering all the places she had once known by heart. Her hungry mouth finding his jaw, his forehead. Legs entwined, bodies moving at that perfect, sweet pace.

And nothing else mattered.

Chapter Fourteen

Sunday, June 11, 9:30 a.m.

"You're sure about this?"

Olivia stared at the man seated in the chair across the table from her…the one who had reminded her last night of all she had lost ten years ago…his touch, the smell of his skin… the taste of his kiss. She never wanted to be far from him again.

Did Huck feel the same way? She couldn't be sure. She'd awakened alone this morning. He'd already gotten up and made coffee. Worse, he seemed somehow distant. Was he ready to bolt again? What had she done to make him feel that need? She understood now that she should have seen his concerns ten years ago. What happened was ultimately both their faults.

She did not want to make the same mistake twice.

"I'm sure." She nodded. "All these secrets

have been kept far too long. I don't want any of this hanging over my head anymore." She shrugged, set her second cup of coffee aside. Going for the extra caffeine felt like a mistake now. She was jumpy…jittery. "We don't have to mention Sheriff Decker's part in all this. I'm sure the ultimate decisions were made by Willy and Gran."

"Decker should have to own his part in this, Liv."

Maybe Huck was right. The truth was she was too close to this to be objective.

"He's your boss—former boss," she finally said. "I'll leave that decision to you."

He nodded. "I'll make some calls. We'll get a team out here to finish the exhumation and collection of the bones."

"Thank you." She met his gaze, wanted to say more, but he gave her a nod and stood.

"I'll be on the porch."

She watched him go, and no matter that he seemed distant or distracted this morning, she was certain she couldn't have read him so wrong last night.

Olivia stood. She needed a walk. If only around the yard. She needed to just soak up the images and scents of home. To brace herself.

Her cell pinged with an incoming text.

Olivia tugged her phone from her pocket and stared at the screen.

Willy.

Her heart bumped into a harder rhythm. The text was from Willy's cell phone. This could be the person who had taken his life. *Breathe,* she told herself as she started toward the front door and simultaneously opened the text.

I need to tell you the real story.

Another text appeared.

It's your mom.

Olivia stalled at the front door, the bottom falling out of her stomach.

Please come to the grave.

Torn between rushing out the back door and telling Huck, her good sense won out and she stepped out onto the porch. Huck was still on the phone. She held her phone in front of his face so he could read the text messages.

His expression shifted to surprise, and his gaze collided with Olivia's. "Thanks, Snelling. Let me know when a team is headed this way."

He lowered the phone from his ear and stood. "You just got those?"

She nodded. "From Willy's phone."

He slid his phone into his pocket and reached for the weapon on the table next to the rocking chair he'd vacated. "Let's go."

Olivia didn't budge. "If it's her and she sees you, she might run."

His head was moving side to side before she finished speaking, his expression hard. "I'm not letting you go alone."

"I know," she agreed. "That's why I'm telling you rather than rushing through the woods right now."

Relief softened his face. "Okay. I'll take the roundabout path, the one we used when we wanted to ditch anyone following us."

She nodded. "I'll take the main path."

"Don't get ahead of me, Liv. Take your time. I'll be able to see you most of the way, but don't get there before I do."

"I won't. I'll take it slow. I'll go out the back, just in case she or whoever is watching."

"I'll give you a thirty-second head start by going through the barn."

She smiled. That was exactly what they used to do when they didn't want Willy and Gran to know they were going to the cliffs. They'd walk leisurely to the barn, slip out the back and barrel through the woods.

"Okay."

He took her by the arm before she could get away. "Be careful."

"You too."

Olivia left the house, strolled along the stone path. She paused at the tree line to send a response.

I'm coming.

Her pulse raced in time with the pounding in her heart. Her mother was out there somewhere. She had no doubt about that now. Whether she was deranged or dangerous, Olivia didn't know. Whether this was even her, she couldn't be sure. But the one thing she felt certain of was that whoever had Willy's phone may have been the person to hurt him.

The thought sent fire rushing through her veins. If her mother had killed Willy, Olivia wasn't sure she could trust herself in the woman's presence. Thank God for Huck.

Rather than get distracted with worries of what the facts might be, she focused on moving forward. She scanned left and right of the path, watching and listening for movement. What if her mother was armed? The thought slowed her steps. Someone had shot the private investigator.

Someone had pushed Willy...

The grave was very close to the cliffs.

Olivia steeled herself and kept moving. She had Huck. If she stopped and looked closely enough, she would see him on that narrow little path they used to take.

Keep moving.

If she looked for him, anyone watching her would notice.

Focus forward.

By the time that big oak came into view, her nerves were jumping. Maybe it was how anxious she felt or some deep instinct that slowed her, but for the first time in a long time she paused to take in the beauty that lay before her.

Past the big tree was the view beyond the cliffs. The sky was clear. It was breathtaking.

"Olivia."

Female voice.

She turned to find a near mirror image standing a few feet away, midway between her and the unearthed bones that now lay in a neat pile rather than spread out as she and Huck had left them.

The woman who was her mother smiled. "You're so beautiful."

She stepped forward. Olivia instinctively stepped back.

Laura's face clouded. "Sorry. I didn't mean to scare you."

Olivia steeled herself. She would not be afraid. She recovered the step she had fallen back, then took another and another until she stood within touching distance of her mother. "I'm not scared."

Laura's smile returned. "I'm glad."

There was nothing in her hands. The jeans she wore fit snuggly, so unless a weapon was hidden behind her, maybe the way Huck sometimes tucked his gun at the small of his back, she wasn't carrying one.

"You wanted to talk," Olivia said rather than the barrage of other things that rushed into her head.

This was her mother.

A dozen turbulent emotions bombarded her at once.

She wasn't dead…why had Gran and Willy lied to her?

Laura's expression shifted to something fierce and bordering on frantic. "You can't trust Decker. He killed your father." Tears welled in her eyes. "He killed Willy."

Olivia stared at her, the fresh sting of pain deep and excruciating. "I don't believe you."

The sheriff and Willy had been friends forever. Why would he do such a thing? He'd even admitted to helping Willy cover up what Laura had done.

"You killed my father. Decker said so."

Laura stared at the ground for a moment. Her shoulders slumped as if she were too weary to hold them straight anymore. Fine strands of gray filtered like tiny silver threads in her dark hair. Her mother was not the smiling, young woman in the photos Olivia's gran had curated. She was much older now. Nearly fifty. She was still beautiful though, her face barely marred by age.

Her mother drew in a deep breath and lifted her face once more. "Whatever he told you was a lie. If you'll let me, I'll tell you the truth."

Olivia nodded. "On one condition."

Her mother searched her face. "What condition?"

"That you allow Huck to be part of this. We can trust him. If what you say is true, he can help you."

The fear in her expression pained Olivia more than she'd anticipated.

"You have my word," Olivia promised. "He would never betray me."

Laura nodded. "If you're sure."

Olivia sent him a text, to keep up the pretense. The longest half a minute Olivia had ever endured later, Huck joined them.

Laura eyed him skeptically at first.

"It's good to see you," he said to her.

She blinked, more tears glistening in her eyes. "Thank you."

The longer Olivia stood there watching her, the more convinced she became that this woman was not in any way unbalanced, but she reserved judgment for now.

"Start at the beginning," Olivia suggested.

Laura nodded. "Daddy and Decker were friends as far back as I can remember." She shrugged. "He was always nice to me. But as I got older, he watched me in a different way." She shuddered. "When I was thirteen, he raped me." She looked away.

Olivia and Huck shared a look. "Can you prove this?" Olivia asked.

Laura shook her head, still looking any-where but at them. "He said the same thing when I told him I was going to tell. He said Willy would never believe me. He had just made chief deputy. Everyone loved him."

Olivia braced herself. "Keep going."

"I stopped fighting it and let him have his way. I lost count of the times. I spent hours fig-uring out ways to avoid being alone anywhere for fear he would show up and make me…" She let go a big breath. "But then I graduated high school and escaped. I was so grateful. I missed Mom and Dad, but the relief of never having that bastard paw me again was worth it." Her expression fell. "Then he caught me away from the university one day, and he did it again. I knew then that I'd never be free of him until I had a man who loved me who might be able to protect me." She smiled. "I met Kasey, and everything was perfect for a while. I got pregnant with you, and we decided to come home. I knew Mom and Dad would help us get on our feet." She closed her eyes for a moment. "I never dreamed he would dare intrude again, but he did."

"He did this to you again?" Olivia said, unable to say the word, her insides twisted into knots.

She nodded. "When you were three." She stared heavenward. "He'd left me alone for three years. I thought it was over. Your dad and I had plans to start an organic farm. We hadn't told Mom and Dad yet, but we'd been traveling around nearby states searching for just the right location. Sometimes we would be gone for a few weeks, but I could never stay gone longer than that." She smiled. "I missed you too much."

Olivia felt undone. "You didn't just disappear all those times?"

Laura frowned. "Who told you that?"

"Decker," Olivia responded, looking from Laura to Huck. No need to mention his mother. She'd only repeated what she'd been told.

The pain on Laura's face tugged at Olivia's heart. She so wanted to believe what this woman—her mother—was telling her. The idea that Willy had trusted Decker made it difficult for Olivia to do otherwise. This woman was a stranger...how could Olivia be certain she was telling the truth?

"He wanted you to believe the same thing he made my parents believe," Laura said. "He twisted their concerns and made them believe things that weren't true. He was so bold that one day I was walking to town and he saw me. He almost ran over me. I ran into the woods, and he parked and came after me." She stared at the ground again. "This time, I told Kasey. He told me to set up a meeting with Decker, and he would take care of it. I did what he said. Decker didn't know Kasey would be there. Kasey told him never to come near me again or else."

"How did Decker respond to the ultimatum?" Huck asked.

Laura jerked at the sound of his voice as

if she'd forgotten he was there. "He…he shot him. I tried to help him." Tears rushed down her cheeks. "He grabbed me, put the gun in my hand and then knocked me unconscious. When I woke up, I was at Pineville. I had been out of it for days. He'd given me some sort of hallucinogenic. My crazy behavior had my parents convinced of his lie that I had killed Kasey. He said we had both been doing drugs. He claimed that the times Kasey left without me were because I had been violent with him. None of that was true. But no matter what I said, no one would believe me. The doctor at Pineville kept me drugged. Finally when I was released, it was weeks before I could get off the meds and pull myself together again. I would try to tell them the truth, but the side effects of withdrawal only convinced them further that I was lying, and I'd end up at Pineville again. It took nearly a year for my brain to get right enough to understand that I would never be free again until I ran away."

"You faked your death," Olivia suggested.

"I was going to," Laura said, "but Decker caught me. He let the note I'd written stand and took me back to Pineville. My parents never knew I was alive."

"Why would Pineville go along?" Huck

asked, his voice telling Olivia he was not convinced.

"The administrator, Leo Rich, and Decker go way back," Laura explained. "I don't know what Decker has on him, but Rich would do whatever Decker said."

"Did you kill Willy?" Olivia demanded.

Laura gasped. "Of course not. I didn't even escape until that bastard told me what he'd done and said if I tried anything else, you would be next."

"What did he mean, try anything else?" Huck asked.

Olivia needed to sit down. She found the nearest boulder and collapsed there.

"I was there for over twenty-five years," she said, her emotions getting the better of her. "Eventually, they stopped keeping me in solitary confinement. I tried making friends with people I knew would be seeing their relatives or be released. I would tell them my story and about my dad. I begged them to get a message to him when they were released, but something always happened. One fell in the shower and hit her head the day before she was to be released. Another hung herself. It was when the third one slit her wrists by digging with her fork until the deed was done that I realized no one could save me. Decker would always find a way to stop me. He and Rich had too many ears in that place."

"You're saying," Olivia spoke up, "this person—this Leo Rich—who did whatever Decker told him killed these people."

Laura nodded. "It's the only explanation."

"But you did eventually escape, obviously," Huck countered.

"It was a long time before I dared. I had resigned myself to dying there." She closed her eyes and shook her head. "I honestly don't know why he didn't kill me a long time ago. I even asked him that on one of his visits."

"He came to see you there?" Olivia's head was spinning.

Laura squared her shoulders. "Numerous times. Said he couldn't bear not to see me. He swore he'd never let me go."

"There are cameras outside the facility," Huck said to Olivia. "If he went there, we can find him on video."

"Knowing him, he will have that figured out too." She stared hard at Huck. "Whatever you believe about Decker, he's capable of anything." She turned back to Olivia. "I spent two years developing a secret friendship. We were so careful. She understood if anyone found out, she would be killed. She was released last Friday. I gave her a necklace—my sunflower necklace—that I always wore so Willy would know she was telling the truth. On Sunday morning, she drove to the cabin and told Willy the truth about where I was and what Decker had done."

"She told you she did this?" Olivia said.

Laura shook her head. "She couldn't risk contacting me back at Pineville. But I know she did because on Monday Decker came to see me. He said he knew what I had done and that my foolishness had caused him to have to kill his best friend—my father. He said if I ever told anyone else or did a single other thing, he would kill you."

Olivia turned to Huck. "I don't know what to believe."

"I knew I had to do something no matter what he said," Laura went on, her voice rising with desperation. "I couldn't trust him to keep his word that he wouldn't touch you as long as I behaved myself. So I took the chance I had been afraid to take all these years." She looked away. "I think I may have hurt one of the attendants pretty badly. I didn't mean to hurt anyone. I just had to get away."

"She may be telling at least part of the truth," Huck said to Olivia.

Olivia held her breath.

"While I was giving you that head start,"

he explained, "Snelling called. Decker's prints were on the wine bottle. Someone had wiped most of them, but there was one perfect print that matched Decker's."

"Decker drinks wine?" Olivia asked.

"Yes," Laura said quickly. "He and I liked the same kind, red."

Huck nodded. "She's right. Me and some of the other deputies used to laugh about having a sheriff who didn't like beer."

"He said they had dinner together on Sunday night," Laura said. "Dad had invited him and then confronted him about what he'd been told. There was a fight, and the injuries Dad got from the fight left Decker no choice but to throw him off Sunset Rock. He thought it was ironic." A sob tore from her throat. "He told me how Dad wanted to kill him for what he'd done, and then he laughed because Dad was the one to die."

"There was a private investigator," Huck said.

Olivia could no longer keep up; tears were streaming down her face, and she felt ready to curl into herself. How had he gotten away with this all these years?

"Decker hired him to find me, and he did," Laura confessed. "I told him the truth, and I think he believed me. Especially because of my father's murder. I think that was maybe the only reason he believed me. The next thing I knew, he was dead too."

"Still telling your lies, I see."

Huck whipped around at the sound of Decker's voice. The weapon pointed directly at his chest kept Huck from reaching for his own.

"Decker," Huck said carefully. "We understand what she's up to," he assured his soon to be former boss. "There's no need for you to prove one damned thing. The woman is obviously insane."

"Huck," Olivia demanded, "what're you doing?"

"I'm not crazy," Laura howled.

"Of course you are," Decker sneered. "I went to a great deal of trouble to show just how nuts you are. Like ransacking Willy's house. Burning down the shed. Taking those photographs." He shook his head. "She was always doing crazy stuff. If Willy and Joyce were here, they would tell you." He laughed. "They never had a clue I was playing them."

"We should get her into custody," Huck suggested, "and clear this up at the station."

Decker laughed. "I know about the prints, so don't try to play games with me, Monroe." He shook his head. "Too bad your crazy mother escaped and killed your lover, Olivia, the same way she killed her husband. And of course, she had to kill you too. Then herself."

"There's just one problem with that," Olivia said. "No one is going to believe you this time, and I think you know it."

Decker laughed. "Maybe. But none of you will be around to corroborate her story."

A guttural howl rent the air. Moving so fast Huck barely saw her, Laura rushed toward Decker.

Decker swung his weapon in her direction.

Huck drew his own.

Gunshots exploded in the air.

Chapter Fifteen

Erlanger Hospital, Chattanooga,
12:00 p.m.

Olivia paced the waiting room.

Her mother was still in surgery. The shot Decker managed to pull off before Huck's shot plowed through his brain had hit its mark. Her mother had been gravely injured.

Laura had been rushed to the hospital with her vitals plummeting.

Olivia wrung her hands, paced the opposite direction. She didn't want her to die. She had just gotten her mother back.

Damn it.

Decker was dead. Thank God.

Acting Sheriff Snelling was executing a warrant at Pineville at this very moment. The last Huck had heard from one of his fellow deputies, the administrator was spilling his guts in hopes of getting some sort of deal. Administrator Leo Rich had accidentally, he claimed, killed a woman when he was in college. Decker had helped him cover up his involvement, and Rich had been paying him back since.

All of it, every single word, made Olivia sick. None of this would bring Willy back, but Olivia was grateful to have found her mother. She had been a prisoner for more than two decades. Laura deserved to have her life back— not to have it taken from her after all she had been through.

Huck came into the small surgery waiting room. "Hey. Any news yet?"

Olivia shook her head. "You?"

"Sergeant Snelling called to say his CSI team found your mother's necklace, along with photos Decker had taken over the years. Several of her in the hospital. Some you don't want to hear about."

Olivia cringed. She hated that bastard. Hoped he rotted in hell.

She steadied herself. "That's more proof she's telling the truth." Olivia felt ill at the idea that her mother had been lost and alone all these years with Willy only a few miles away.

The whole thing was insane.

The door opened and the surgeon, still wearing surgical scrubs, walked in.

Olivia's knees felt weak. Huck was suddenly at her side, his arm around her back.

"Your mother came through well," he said. "She'll need some time to heal, but I expect a full recovery."

Relief gushed through Olivia. "Thank you. When can I see her?"

"She'll be in recovery for an hour or so, and then we'll get her settled into a room. You can see her then."

Olivia thanked him again. When the door closed behind the doctor, she turned to Huck. "Thank you for all you've done. I wouldn't have gotten through this without you. I'm certain I wouldn't have found the truth without you."

Confusion lined his handsome face. "I'm concerned this sounds like goodbye."

Olivia smiled. "I will have to go back to Bozeman and pack up my townhouse. Settle things at my office. But then I'll be back."

It was impossible to miss the hope in his eyes. "For good?"

She shrugged. "Or bad, depending on how you look at it. You see, Deputy Detective Monroe, if I'm staying here, it has to be a package deal."

His eyebrows went up. "Package deal?"

"I get you in the deal."

"I'm more than happy to oblige, ma'am."

He kissed her to seal the best deal of their lives.

Deep in her heart, Olivia had always known there was no place like home.

* * * * *

Get 3 FREE REWARDS!

We'll send you 2 FREE Books plus a FREE Mystery Gift.

FREE Value Over **$20**

Both the **Harlequin Intrigue®** and **Harlequin® Romantic Suspense** series feature compelling novels filled with heart-racing action-packed romance that will keep you on the edge of your seat.

YES! Please send me 2 FREE novels from the Harlequin Intrigue or Harlequin Romantic Suspense series and my FREE gift (gift is worth about $10 retail). After receiving them, if I don't wish to receive any more books, I can return the shipping statement marked "cancel." If I don't cancel, I will receive 6 brand-new Harlequin Intrigue Larger-Print books every month and be billed just $6.49 each in the U.S. or $6.99 each in Canada, a savings of at least 13% off the cover price, or 4 brand-new Harlequin Romantic Suspense books every month and be billed just $5.49 each in the U.S. or $6.24 each in Canada, a savings of at least 12% off the cover price. It's quite a bargain! Shipping and handling is just 50¢ per book in the U.S. and $1.25 per book in Canada.* I understand that accepting the 2 free books and gift places me under no obligation to buy anything. I can always return a shipment and cancel at any time by calling the number below. The free books and gift are mine to keep no matter what I decide.

Choose one:
☐ **Harlequin Intrigue Larger-Print** (199/399 BPA GRMX) ☐ **Harlequin Romantic Suspense** (240/340 BPA GRMX) ☐ **Or Try Both!** (199/399 & 240/340 BPA GRQD)

Name (please print)

Address   Apt. #

City   State/Province   Zip/Postal Code

Email: Please check this box ☐ if you would like to receive newsletters and promotional emails from Harlequin Enterprises ULC and its affiliates. You can unsubscribe anytime.

Mail to the Harlequin Reader Service:
IN U.S.A.: P.O. Box 1341, Buffalo, NY 14240-8531
IN CANADA: P.O. Box 603, Fort Erie, Ontario L2A 5X3

Want to try 2 free books from another series? Call 1-800-873-8635 or visit www.ReaderService.com.

*Terms and prices subject to change without notice. Prices do not include sales taxes, which will be charged (if applicable) based on your state or country of residence. Canadian residents will be charged applicable taxes. Offer not valid in Quebec. This offer is limited to one order per household. Books received may not be as shown. Not valid for current subscribers to the Harlequin Intrigue or Harlequin Romantic Suspense series. All orders subject to approval. Credit or debit balances in a customer's account(s) may be offset by any other outstanding balance owed by or to the customer. Please allow 4 to 6 weeks for delivery. Offer available while quantities last.

Your Privacy—Your information is being collected by Harlequin Enterprises ULC, operating as Harlequin Reader Service. For a complete summary of the information we collect, how we use this information and to whom it is disclosed, please visit our privacy notice located at corporate.harlequin.com/privacy-notice. From time to time we may also exchange your personal information with reputable third parties. If you wish to opt out of this sharing of your personal information, please visit readerservice.com/consumerschoice or call 1-800-873-8635. **Notice to California Residents**—Under California law, you have specific rights to control and access your data. For more information on these rights and how to exercise them, visit corporate.harlequin.com/california-privacy.

HIHRS23

Get 3 FREE REWARDS!

We'll send you 2 FREE Books plus a FREE Mystery Gift.

Get 3 FREE REWARDS!

We'll send you 2 FREE Books plus a FREE Mystery Gift.